widows

widows

a novel

ARIEL DORFMAN

Translated from the Spanish
by Stephen Kessler

SEVEN STORIES PRESS
New York · Toronto · London · Sydney

First published in the United States of America by Pantheon Books, a division of Random House, Inc., 1983

First Seven Stories Press Edition September 2002

Seven Stories Press
140 Watts Street
New York, NY 10013
http://www.sevenstories.com

In Canada: Hushion House, 36 Northline Road, Toronto, Ontario M4B 3E2

In the U.K.: Turnaround Publisher Services Ltd., Unit 3, Olympia Trading Estate, Coburg Road, Wood Green, London N22 6TZ

In Australia: Tower Books, 2/17 Rodborough Road, Frenchs Forest NSW 2086

Library of Congress Cataloging-in-Publication Data
Dorfman, Ariel.
[Viudas. English]
Widows : a novel / Ariel Dorfman ; translated from the Spanish by Stephen Kessler. — 1st Seven Stories Press ed.
p. cm.
ISBN 1-58322-483-1 (pbk.)
I. Kessler, Stephen, 1947– II. Title.
PQ8098.14.O7 V513 2002
863'.64—dc21

2002008915

9 8 7 6 5 4 3 2 1

College professors may order examination copies of Seven Stories Press titles for a free six-month trial period. To order, visit www.sevenstories.com/textbook, or fax on school letterhead to (212) 226-1411.

Book design by M. Astella Saw

Printed in Canada

by way of dedication

I was going to publish this novel under another name.

If I sought to hide its true father, it was not because I was ashamed of the son, but because books with my name on them could not—and many still cannot—circulate freely in Chile and the other countries of the southern cone of Latin America. But there was another reason as well: The novel I was planning dealt with the disappearance of thousands of men, and some women, into the hands of the secret police of those dictatorships. Taken from their homes in the dead of night or abducted in open daylight on the streets, these people are never seen again. Their relatives are left not just without their loved ones, but without any certainty about whether they are alive or dead. The "missing" are deprived of more than their homes, their livelihoods, their children. They are also deprived of their graves. It's as if they had never existed. A novel about this sort of situation was not the kind that would endear a publisher to the authorities, the very authorities who had the power to make him too disappear.

My body had already been banned from those countries. I didn't want my new book to be banned as well, so I decided to write a story that apparently took place in Greece, at a somewhat undefined period of the twentieth century, and publish it under a name I had invented, Eric Lohmann. I hoped readers would be persuaded that it had indeed been penned forty years ago in Denmark, just before the author himself was taken off into the "nacht und nebel."

My plan was that we would first bring the book out in Danish or German or French, and then have it "translated" into Spanish. Several prominent writer friends were ready to offer support by writing introductions or lending their names as "translators," so that my child might grow up where it belonged, in its true land, among its own. The scheme was not as farfetched as it may sound.

The inmates of the Chilean concentration camps had managed to exhibit plays which they had written themselves, by the simple method of attributing them to nonexistent, foreign authors. If they could do that from behind barbed wire, why couldn't I do something similar from my own position of relative freedom.

Before beginning, however, I contacted a publishing house of some importance that had no problem putting out books in those countries. The editor-in-chief took an enthusiastic interest in the project, but wouldn't commit himself until he could read the manuscript. His only suggestion was that maybe I should "go easy" on the military characters. Maybe it was because I didn't listen to him, maybe it was for other reasons, but when I finally delivered the completed version, the company chose not to risk printing the book; and if they didn't dare, I knew no one else would even look at it.

I hadn't expected that decision, and it left me in a rather curious situation. It made no sense to publish the novel under its pseudonym, since access to the readers I wanted to reach was blocked anyway. But it didn't seem right either to redo the narrative, giving it a contemporary, more realistic Latin American framework and atmosphere. I liked the novel as it was. By forcing myself to choose my words with caution, by forcing myself to witness such a traumatic and immediate experience from a distance, by forcing myself to explore a language which could not be traced to the style that Latin American readers and critics might have recognized as my own, it seemed to me I had managed to make the plight of the missing people into something more universal, which could happen anywhere, at any time, to anyone. It is our misfortune that it is happening today in my own Chile, in El Salvador, in South Africa, in the Philippines. It happened in Denmark yesterday, and who knows where it will happen tomorrow. Just a little imagination is needed to shift the characters and change the landscape.

But there was another reason why I did not want to modify that manuscript. As I watched the words spill out, I came to identify more and more with its dead European author, listening to his tenderness, possessed by his rage to endure. In the end all that was left for me to do was to give over to the reader, who someday soon may also be of that southern cone, this novel for which I take responsibility.

This way, whoever reads the book can judge whether it also could have been written—and it was, nobody has to certify it so—by that Danish resistance fighter, that brother forty years my senior, that father who never got to meet his son, to whose memory I dedicate these pages he managed to finish a few days before his death, before they came to get him, the same men who years later, on another continent, keep coming and coming to take men and women away from their families.

ARIEL DORFMAN
Washington, D.C.
September 1982

widows

a novel by

Eric Lohmann

foreword by the author's son

I never met my father. Men from the Gestapo came for him in April 1942, one month before my birth. Perhaps my mother's advanced condition had something to do with their not taking her away too. "It's a routine interrogation," they told her, but she knew that wasn't so, that she'd never see Father again. After the war, over a period of months, my mother questioned former inmates of the concentration camps where Danes were habitually sent, but no one had ever seen him.

Only years later, when I began asking my mother more specific questions about the man whose picture I had always had beside my bed, did I find out about the novel. In the months preceding his arrest and disappearance, really from the moment he knew for certain that someone like me was on the way, my father set out in his spare time to write a work of fiction. I'm told he joked about it, saying he'd already planted so many trees, and now that a child was about to bless our turbulent world the only thing lacking was to write a book, and in times like these it had to be done fast, because one never knew how much time was left. It appears that he managed to finish the first draft a few weeks before the Gestapo squadron came to get him, but my mother never read it and didn't even know where the manuscript had gone. She assumed, naturally enough, that it had been lost or had ended up in the possession of some obscure colonel of the secret police.

Recently, however, we recovered the novel, after its being missing for some thirty-odd years. A cousin of mine found it in the bottom of a trunk full of old papers and periodicals, as she was preparing to move from the huge country house that was now too big for her family now that her children had married. We figured that my father had delivered the manuscript to his sister, my aunt Gertrudis, whose judgment (they were twins) he deemed faultless. We know that she became gravely ill a few weeks later, almost exactly at the moment of my father's arrest, and no doubt had neither the time nor the energy to inform my mother or anyone else about the novel. When my aunt died soon thereafter, no one again disturbed those papers in all those years.

The novel came preceded by a brief letter addressed to my mother and to the son or daughter about to be born, asking them, in case anything happened, to see to its publication, as it was, but under a pseudonym. He thought, of course, that it would have to be circulated illegally. His insistence on the use of a false name arose, I'm sure, from the belief that the Nazi occupation would continue for a prolonged period. Or maybe it simply had to do with an excessive modesty or shyness, character traits which his friends have mentioned to me. Be that as it may, we've decided to carry out his wishes and publish the novel, under a pseudonym, despite its fragmentary character. (We don't even know if it's missing some parts, as seems to be the case with section ten.) We feel this is an act of respect for his memory.

The publishers desired, nevertheless, that the author's son should clarify the circumstances of the novel's origins, which explain some peculiarities that might not otherwise be comprehensible.

As the reader will see, the action occurs in a country that resembles Greece, although it is never named as such. But the historical situation described here has nothing to do with what was happening in Greece at that time. The Greek Quisling government did not maintain its own army, as did Denmark, although its police force and a few groups of shock troops did help with the mop-up work during the German occupation. My father's novel seems, if anything, more like an unusual mixture of two previous epochs in Greek twentieth-century history—the Metaxas dictatorship and the foreign invasion that followed. Clearly, though, what my father did was to transport to a country like Greece a story that could just as well have happened in Denmark, had our country had mountains and a Balkan guerrilla tradition.

According to my mother, my father never visited Greece or any other Mediterranean country. He set his novel in that distant realm, which suffered a similar tragedy, the better to comment on what was occurring around him. The Norwegian and Danish events that he knew so well were perhaps too close to home to contain his visions.

It may be that this distancing explains one of the greatest merits, in my judgment, of his work. The country he created is not Greece but an imaginary place equivalent to all Europe of that epoch. Written between 1941 and 1942, the novel presages what was to occur in his own country, in Holland, in France, in Italy, in Poland, in the years to come. But more than that, it announces what was to happen in Greece itself after the Second World War, during the civil war. Beyond that, it prefigures what is still happening now, decades later, in so many areas of the Third World.

I hope, as does my mother, that the publication of this book may contribute, even in the smallest way, toward the prevention of what is told here ever happening again.

My father had the capacity to understand, absorb, and express the grief of his widow and of the son who never knew him. It is worthwhile asking today what the talent and tenderness of my father might have produced had he not disappeared into the hands of the men who came that night to take him away.

SIRGUD LOHMANN

the family

Sofia Angelos

Karoulos Mylonas, *her father*

Michael Angelos, *her husband*

Dimitriou Angelos, *her elder son*

Serguei, *her younger son*

Hilda, *her sister*

Cristina, Rosa, Maria, *her unmarried daughters*

Alexandra, *Dimitriou's wife*

Fidelia and Alexis, twins, *the daughter and son of Dimitriou and Alexandra*

Yanina, *Serguei's wife*

Little Serguei, *the son of Serguei and Yanina*

chapter one

⸿ i ⸿

"That old bitch again?" said the captain. "Again?"

"Yes, sir. The same one."

"The same one. That's what I was afraid of. Tell her I'm not in."

"I already told her that, sir. I told her you weren't in."

"Well?"

"With your permission, Captain, she says she'll wait until you come out."

"But didn't you tell her I wasn't in? Isn't that what you said?"

"She says she'll wait, that there's only one door and that you'll have to come out where you went in. That's what she said, Captain."

"And the body? It's about the body, right?"

"It's still there, Captain."

"And the women?"

"The same, Captain. They're still there, next to the river."

"It must be about the body, the son of a bitch. Another body. It must be about that, don't you think?"

"If you say so, Captain."

"'If you say so, if you say so.' Don't you have any opinions of your own? Can't you speak and think for yourself? If you say so, if I say so. I'm asking you what you think."

"Yes, sir, it must be about the body. The lady claims it's Michael Angelos. That she's the wife."

Before responding, the captain took out a cigarette and lit it.

"Wife? She's this one's wife?"

"That's what she claims, Captain."

"How can she know she's the wife if she hasn't even seen it?"

"I don't know, sir. Ask her, if you want to."

"She hasn't even been to the river, right?"

"No, she hasn't, Captain. As soon as she found out about the body, she came straight here. Just like the other time."

The captain got up and walked to the window. The spotless window was the only clean thing for miles. Outside, even at this early hour, the heat was drying, twisting, tightening the air. A little girl passed with a donkey. The two went by slowly and disappeared. The dust they'd raised came down, taking its time, swirling to the ground. It was as if no one had ever walked down the street.

"Stink hole." The captain bit off the words under his breath. "I have to be posted to this fucking stink hole. You're from around here, aren't you?" He already knew the answer. Captain Gheorghakis had given him the details before leaving him in charge of the unit. And Philip Kastoria, the owner of almost all this land, who lived on the far side of the mountains, had also recommended the orderly with special enthusiasm. But during the last two weeks he hadn't wanted to formulate this question, hadn't wanted to admit any disorientation in this inhospitable, unknown spot. Now it came out naturally.

"From the area, Captain. I was born about forty miles from here, on the other side of the hill. I was employed by Mr. Kastoria. Perhaps they told you."

The captain waited for him to continue, but the orderly offered no more particulars. "Forty miles," the captain repeated, swallowing the heat and the violent light coming through the window, those blind white walls under the sun, the rickety cypresses covered with a fine white dust awaiting the slightest blessing of a breeze, even the shadows chalky. "So you understand them, you understand these people—or don't you?"

"Sort of, Captain."

"Sort of?"

"I'm different from them, Captain. With your permission, Captain, but I don't think I'll stay here my whole life."

The captain didn't turn around.

"So this is a fucking stink hole for you too?"

"I wouldn't live here my whole life, sir, if that's what you mean."

"Okay, for now, you're going to do two things. First you're going to turn on the fan. That's the first thing you'll do. And second you're going to go out and advise that old bitch that I'm not going to see her because I don't have time, that I'm busy today and tomorrow too. And you're going to convince her that it would be nice if she went home and tended her sheep or whatever, because that way I won't have to dirty my boots. Understood?"

"Yes, sir."

The orderly went to the desk and put on the fan. The captain heard the hum of the motor and a few seconds later felt the fleeting satisfaction of a little gust of warm air hitting his sweaty shoulders. He turned decisively, his hands behind his back, and walked over to the desk.

Just then the orderly opened the door. For an instant the captain caught a glimpse of the figure in black sunk in a corner of the improvised anteroom, and remembered that look with which she'd observed him throughout their first and only interview, just the day after he'd arrived to take charge of the regiment. It seemed unreal, the two weeks since then, two weeks in this rotting, forgotten town. He was going to have to take a day off to visit the Kastorias and enjoy a little taste of civilization. He couldn't live like this.

The door closed.

He conjured up an image of the stubborn old woman. She'd probably leave the building and install herself a few steps away, wait there all morning, all afternoon, all night, like the other time, without moving an inch, still as a statue, a piece of rubbish scarcely stirring. That old woman and all the old women like her ought to be dead, ought to be stacked like stones in the cemetery.

"And that old woman?" the captain had asked, two weeks ago, when he'd passed her on the way in, then on the way out, then on the way in again.

"She's been here two days, Captain. Says she wants to see you." She hadn't acknowledged the reference. She was simply there, facing the door of the headquarters, vigilant, her mouth pressed tight, entirely submerged in her black dress, as if she hadn't slept all night.

"We'll clear this up in a hurry." The captain said it loudly, so all his subordinates could hear. "What do you want?" he'd demanded, brutal, to the point, ready to set things straight at a single stroke.

"I want to bury my father. My father, Karoulos Mylonas."

"Then bury him. What have I got to do with it?"

"The soldiers already did," she said in a monotone, without raising her eyes, as if the captain wasn't going to believe her anyway.

The captain hesitated for an instant. He was aware of the stiff orderly beside him, the sergeant and the two guards at the entrance. It wasn't the time to find out the history of the case. He had to show he was in control, absolute control, now.

He strode into the anteroom with two huge steps, coming to the door of his own office. From there he turned around and gestured indifferently to the woman to follow him. He crossed the threshold decisively. While he was making himself comfortable in his chair, she had come in, dragging herself like a shadow.

"All right," said the captain. "He's buried then. So you've got nothing to worry about."

"No," she said, and he waited for the next word, a little more, but that negation hung there alone and echoless. The woman had nothing more to explain.

"I don't understand." The captain was getting impatient. "Is your father buried or isn't he?"

"The soldiers buried him, but I didn't."

"You weren't present?"

"Just the soldiers."

All of a sudden the captain realized what bothered him about this old woman, besides the nasty little mustache growing irritably on her lip, besides that little bend of the head that gave her gaze a special, malignant gleam. It was that she never blinked. He'd never seen her shut her eyes for a second: they were open, bigger than you'd have expected in a person that age. In the middle of those wrinkled sockets, they burned with a quiet fury, protruding from the black shawl, the wasted skin, and those petrified lids.

"And you wished to be present, that's what you're trying to tell me."

"The soldiers," she said, very deliberately, "had no right to bury my father."

The captain suddenly realized he didn't just feel confused. He also felt—it was impossible, where could such a sensation come from?—threatened, as if someone here or elsewhere were playing a trick on him. The father of this woman would have to be at least seventy, maybe older. It wasn't the sort of problem the army would worry about. He rang the bell with nervous authority.

"Captain?"

He studied the orderly. According to Gheorghakis, he was worth his weight in gold. Knows the quirks of the local population, a man well trusted by Philip Kastoria, consult him on anything. Never failed me, peasants don't like him, but born around here, aware of what goes on in these savages' heads.

"Call Lieutenant Constantopoulos."

The orderly looked briefly at the woman, then the captain, and saluted. Was there a faint smile on his mouth? The captain chose to ignore it. He lacked the confidence to ask for information when he'd only been in command one day. Later, perhaps, he'd see about that.

He said to the woman, "We're going to consult the lieutenant."

She didn't answer. But he wasn't willing to leave things like that. He wanted to zero in on this matter. "Because you're not going to tell me that you had no time to prepare your father's burial."

"I told Captain Gheorghakis. But he didn't pay any attention. He ordered him buried like a nobody."

The captain decided to ignore her.

He busied himself with the reports on his desk. Actually, the situation was quite calm. There had been no confrontations lately. The mop-up procedures were almost finished. The regime's few adversaries, the ones still scattered about, seemed to have ceased their activities. Once more he read the analysis with which Captain Gheorghakis had concluded his report. Subversion was slowly moving to the cities or the larger towns, though it was just possible that the next weeks might register a last recurrence of violent acts and perhaps small meetings in out-of-the-way towns and villages. You could never be sure about the tactics the enemy might come up with. In any case, he had left the new commander a region secure from all armed terrorism, a region governed with an iron hand, well patrolled, a population with no alternative but to obey, actual and potential centers of rebellion eliminated, the military situation under control. It was the new captain's job—in accordance with the general plan of the Supreme Government—to win the sympathies of the residents, begin a constructive phase of social and economic development, possible only now that the disruptive elements had been bled white by one defeat after another.

"Good morning, Captain. With your permission."

Lieutenant Constantopoulos appeared in his spotless uniform, not sweating a drop, stiff as an arrow. He looked like his father. It was amazing how much he resembled the general. Even now one could see the stern features of that military family, the innate gift of command springing from his hands, from his powerful squared shoulders, from the efficient mathematical rap of his boots against the floor.

"Good morning, Lieutenant."

"You called for me, Captain?"

The officer's colorless eyes hadn't even grazed the figure in black, that woman standing in the same stubborn spot where she'd stopped on coming in. You'd have said she was sculpted in black stone if it weren't for those fixed and burning eyes, and also those lips that moved on their own when she spoke, independent, puppetlike.

The captain gestured smoothly in her direction, as if to say, And this, what can you tell me about this? "This lady's come to file a complaint concerning the burial of her father. Perhaps you'd be good enough to explain this matter to me."

The lieutenant's voice boomed—harsh, decisive, disinterested. "It's not her father, Captain. It wasn't even a relative."

The captain scrutinized her to see how she'd react, but it was as if she'd heard the words before and now it made no sense to waste time listening or responding to them. That's how these people saved their energy. They'd learned to do only what was absolutely necessary in order to survive in this heat, this sterile terrain.

"All right, all right," the captain barked half playfully. "What do you say about that?"

Suddenly, the old woman executed a totally unexpected maneuver. Without a word, she sat down in the chair facing the desk, putting the lieutenant behind her and a little to the right. Then she pulled the chair a few inches closer and leaned toward the captain. When she spoke, her voice was low. It was clear that she didn't want the lieutenant to hear, although her raspy tones could be caught even in the anteroom.

"Do you think, Captain, that I can't recognize my own father?"

The lieutenant quickly intervened. "The body was discovered floating in the river. The women found it at dawn when they went to do their washing. It was totally unrecognizable. Not a clue to its identity."

"Fingerprints?" asked the captain, although he was thinking of other things, and the question was more or less automatic.

"A prolonged stay in the water, Captain."

"And the facial features couldn't be distinguished?" the captain muttered slowly, unable to take his eyes off the old woman.

"The body and the face were badly battered by the river rocks, Captain. It had been exposed for several days. Someone must have dumped it in upriver, for reasons unknown to us."

"And the corpse showed no other signs of violence?"

The lieutenant pointed toward a set of reports the captain had not yet opened. "It's all accounted for in there, sir. Captain Gheorghakis decided, since we couldn't clearly identify the deceased, to bury him as soon as possible in order to prevent contamination and other potential dangers."

"And her?"

"The lady here asked for an interview with Captain Gheorghakis, who graciously agreed to the request. She declared, to our surprise, that the deceased was her father and that she wished to bury him. However, she provided no additional proof of the truth of her assertion. Captain Gheorghakis had no choice but to reject her claim. With your permission, sir, he felt he might be dealing with a subversive attempt to rally opponents of the regime, converting the body of some unknown vagabond into a martyr or hero."

"Of course," agreed the captain firmly. "Or perhaps the guerrillas were settling accounts among themselves. As always, when they're beaten. That happened in my region."

"That's how it was interpreted, sir. In times like these we couldn't risk a normal funeral."

"All right, all right." The captain set down the report and folded his hands, clutching his fingers together until they were white. "And what do you say to this, madam?"

"I lived with my father all my life, Captain."

The captain stood up impetuously. He felt big, was conscious of the smart shine of his boots, his muscles and nerves alive, his belt taut, his lungs drawing smoothly, his uniform a perfect fit. "And if you loved your father so much," said the captain, "why didn't you take better care of him? Why weren't you by his side at the time of his death?"

With a quickness no one had anticipated, the old woman pulled a locket from her black dress. It held a faded turn-of-the-century photo. She set it on the table, taking care not to let go of its chain. She clutched that chain as if it were a trigger.

"This," she said, as if it were explanation enough, "is my father."

The captain looked the portrait over without much interest. A young peasant like so many others, immortalized in a solemn moment. It was even difficult to establish a family resemblance. At that many years' remove, what could there be but some vaguely familiar air? Of course, there was always the possibility of joking with the lieutenant over the only visible similarity, the mustache, which in the father's case was thicker and bushier.

"This photo," the old woman stated abruptly, "was taken the day I was born."

The captain let a growing exasperation color his tone of voice. "Explain to me, then, how it's possible that a man that age could appear in the river, just tell me that. What was your father up to that he should end up, according to you, tossed in a river?"

The old woman picked up the locket but didn't close it or put it away. Hanging from that bony hand, it balanced in the air as if swayed by a secret breeze.

The captain followed the swinging for an instant.

"They took him away from me, sir. They took him away one night, saying they'd bring him back in a few hours. It's more than a year since then, sir."

The lieutenant interrupted. The resonance of his words left no room for argument. "This Mylonas was a notoriously dangerous element, Captain. He used to speak in the taverns, in the cafés, in the market. He was repeatedly warned that what he was saying could cause him problems. Given his age, nothing ever happened. Nonetheless, one day his family appeared before a judge and denounced the disappearance of the gentleman in question. They said he had been abducted. To a written inquiry from the court, Captain Gheorghakis responded that in this unit we had no news concerning the disappearance of anyone who answered to that description." The lieutenant indicated the locket, the portrait, the face that had been captured nearly half a century ago. The old woman hastily put the locket back inside her shawl. "After that we paid no attention to the matter. As you know from your own experience, these sorts of people often use similar methods to carry out clandestine activities. They disappear for a while. Later they kill each other, or attack the police force, or suffer some accident, and then they try to implicate the government. Or our allies."

The captain opened the top drawer of the desk. His eyes rested for an instant on a photo of a woman with three children, his wife waiting for him in the capital. Then he took out a sheaf of papers and shut the drawer.

"Do you know what this is, ma'am? This is the new amnesty decree. It's just been enacted. If your father has had problems with the government in the past, he has nothing to fear. This law allows him to surrender without any further inconvenience."

The voice of the old woman came to them from some other time, some other throat, as if she were repeating something that had been expressed already to no purpose, that she or someone else would have to establish again some unknown day, in this country or another.

"I explained to the judge that we sold a goat in order to make the journey. I explained to him, at that age, tell me, at his age, do you think he'd go off into the hills climbing around and playing tricks like a young man? You might as well accuse me of being dangerous, me, a good Christian who minds my own business and doesn't get mixed up in politics."

The troublesome old bitch! She was managing to put him in the position of arbitrator, making him decide between the lieutenant's version and hers. She was shrewder than she looked. He should have taken Gheorghakis's advice. He should have confided more in the orderly. Now it was necessary to settle the matter. Right here. Right away.

"Mrs. Angelos. The army's duty is to serve the public. We try to maintain the best relations possible with the populace. But I must advise you that I'm very busy. I've just arrived at this post and there are urgent matters to attend to. Tell me once and for all, what do you want me to do? Why did you come to see me?"

The old woman stood and walked to the door. From there, taking leave, knowing he would deny it, she said, "Very simple, sir. I want your soldiers to give me back the body."

"To give it back? Dig it up?"

She gave a half nod.

The captain had then, in that moment two weeks before, raised his voice and half winked at the lieutenant out of the corner of his eye as if to whisper, This is what I get for dealing with crazy old ladies, but not again, I swear to you never again.

"Captain Gheorghakis made a decision on the matter, which I respect and support. Listen. Your father is probably alive. Imagine him arriving in town tomorrow and being told that the army had sanctioned such madness. It's not possible, do you understand. You can't mix our religion up with that kind of witchcraft."

"It's clear, Captain"—the old woman breathed hard—"it's clear that you are no Christian." She looked him up and down with those coal-like unblinking eyes. "I'm going to tell you something, Captain." She shook a long finger in the direction of the window. "Out there in the cemetery, on the hill, there's a grave, my mother's. Karoulos Mylonas, my father, deserves a funeral that God would smile on, sir, a regular funeral. It doesn't matter to me how long I have to wait, someday I'm going to give it to him. I'm going to bury him with a priest and with his name. With all the letters of the name he gave me before I married and had children. Up there, on the hill, in the cemetery, next to my mother's grave, that's where I'm going to bury him."

She shut the door and was gone.

"Just wait," the lieutenant said, after a pause. "She didn't even tell you about the rest of the family."

"The rest? What rest?"

"The rest of the family. The men, at least. Six months before what happened to her father, it so happens her husband and two sons were taken away. They haven't turned up yet either."

The captain scrutinized the closed door as if the old woman was still standing there. He took out his pack of cigarettes and offered one to the lieutenant, who declined, muttering with a half smile, No thanks, not me, but thanks anyway.

"Six months before." The captain lit up. "Then I guess we'll have to forgive these outbursts. For the moment. What do you say, Lieutenant?"

The lieutenant said nothing.

⟨ ii ⟩

About a hundred yards from the river, where a path starts down, the lieutenant found the doctor waiting. The doctor was smoking quietly, in the shade of a short but wide-branching cypress, trying to catch a glimpse, through the smoke, of the river murmuring along nearby and the group of women waiting below.

"I thought I'd hold off," said the doctor, snuffing out the butt and getting up.

"You don't seem to be in much of a hurry," the lieutenant observed. "But dead men don't run away, so why should we worry?"

"A second body in the same place. I can't believe it."

"You'll believe it," said the lieutenant, "when you touch it. Let's go."

He signaled the four soldiers to head down first.

The women—there must have been eight or nine of them—stayed at a certain distance from the corpse, forming something like a wary, irregular semicircle. They were all in mourning, except for one young girl, all motionless as if they were shrubs that someone had planted here centuries ago anticipating this moment: the body of a man facedown on this beach of stones. When the lieutenant, the doctor, and the four soldiers approached within twenty paces, the whole group came alive, a wave of slow movement like water flowing into a pond, finding its level, like a ripple with no beginning or end.

The lieutenant stepped out ahead, leading the way.

"Full of surprises, this river," he said quite loudly. "I don't suppose anyone's moved the body, right?" And since none of them answered, he repeated the question more emphatically: Had anyone moved the body, yes or no?

The women shook their heads no.

"And which one of you found it?"

There was an inclusive, total, multiple gesture indicating all and none, a restrained dance of hands, shoulders, linked black skirts against the line of the river, a motion that ran through them and then stopped. All, they'd all found it together this morning.

The doctor squatted beside the body. Without even touching it, he said, "He's dead, no doubt about it. It's been several days, at least."

"Doctor," said the lieutenant, "we can all see that. I hope you can give us a little more specific information."

"It has to be turned over."

"All right. Go ahead."

The doctor called on one of the soldiers and showed him the direction in which he wanted the body turned.

The women said nothing when they saw the face, when they saw the pulp that had once been its face, decayed and wasted by the pounding and soaking.

"Hey, you." The lieutenant suddenly called the girl, the only one in the group who stood out because she wasn't wearing black. "Come over here."

The girl came a little closer, head down, eyes hidden, eclipsed.

"Did you all get a look at the face? Did you look at the corpse's face?"

"I don't know, sir," said the girl.

"You don't know? How come? Didn't you find the body, you and these others?"

"No, sir. They called for me later."

"Who called for you?"

The girl indicated a woman to her left, identical to the rest, except perhaps a little heartier in the shoulders, a little less grief-worn.

The lieutenant went up to her. "You found the body?"

The woman didn't answer. Her attention hovered and focused on the doctor's hands, which were beginning to undress the dead man, feeling around and exploring as they tore at its clothes with the soldier's help.

"Answer. Did you find it?"

The woman nodded without taking her eyes off the technical, efficient fingers of the doctor. "Yes, sir. Along with the others, sir."

"And you all looked at the face. Could you recognize it?"

She wavered. The doctor had uncovered the man's torso. Incredibly, on that gashed-out chest, with its torn blue skin, its broken rib cage, you could still see hair, hair abundantly covering the arms and trunk.

"I think that's enough," said the doctor. "There's no need to take the pants off."

"Take them off," said the lieutenant.

"It's not necessary for the preliminary examination."

"Take them off. It'll help identify him. You know, in these cases..."

"We didn't want to," the woman said suddenly.

"You didn't want to see his face?"

"No, sir. The other time..."

"Were you the one who discovered the other one too?"

She motioned toward the group.

For a few minutes it was quiet. The lieutenant looked at the doctor's brisk hands, at the stunned women in their semicircle, as if they were watching a theatrical work or acting in it, motionless, letting the light morning breeze contribute the only other movement, fluttering among those long lethargic skirts, revealing for a second the shape of a thigh, an ankle, some way in.

"And so, Doctor, what do you say? Can you determine the cause of death?"

The doctor didn't rise or even raise his eyes. He kept poking around. "Without an autopsy it's hard to make any diagnosis that wouldn't be provisional, Lieutenant. Water in the lungs, things like that. But he's been beaten badly enough to have killed him several times over."

"The river?"

"Not just the river," said the doctor, digging with his fingers. "Burns, swelling, contusions, broken bones—a disaster. It looks to me like he was given a good beating before they dumped him in. And the deceased was quite hungry, Lieutenant. Take a good look at these ribs, the cheekbones," and he ran his fingers over these parts as if giving an anatomy lesson.

"I think the river is mainly responsible, Doctor," the lieutenant gently suggested. "Don't you think so?"

"I already told you what I think." The doctor stood up. "But if you think otherwise, I'm no one to oppose your opinion."

"I think otherwise. And you're right, you're no one. You're simply serving the fatherland's army for a year because we need you quacks."

"Without an autopsy, without the necessary instruments..."

"There's no need for an autopsy."

"If you say so."

"As a matter of fact, I do. What about the subject's identity? Any clues?"

"About fifty years old, more or less. A peasant. Curly dark hair. Color of eyes impossible to tell at this point, but we can assume they were also dark. Skin tanned by the sun, lots of sun, a peasant, look at those hands. A poor man. Quite hungry toward the end, as I said. Anything else?"

"And in his pockets?"

"Nothing."

The lieutenant moved closer to the body. It was totally unrecognizable. What was needed now was to formalize the identification process. The women should pass alongside the dead man so there'd be no misunderstandings later, no claims, no one asking to bury the body like the first time.

They filed by in silence, kneeling next to the man thrown face-up on the rocks, crossing themselves before and after, praying in some inaudible litany. Then they returned to their places. Only the girl stayed out of this ritual, only she remained off to the side, consumed by something that could have been terror or sadness or a distant disgust for the dead man.

"So no one?" asked the lieutenant.

A woman stepped forward. She was pale and breathed with difficulty. Her hands flew up nervously, like captive birds, gesturing in the air.

"It could be my brother, sir."

"Your brother?" The lieutenant raised his eyebrows in amazement. "Could it be?"

"They took him away eight months ago, sir. It could be him."

"But you can't be sure, right? Or do you recognize him?"

Her hands were wringing like twin shadows smashed together, fusing and denying each other under the sun. "How could I be sure, sir? How could I want this to be my brother?"

"Fine. It's clear, then. You don't recognize him. And nobody else recognizes him either. It's clear as can be."

"Shall we take it away, Lieutenant?" asked one of the soldiers.

Just then the girl spoke. She hadn't moved from the spot where the lieutenant had left her.

"It's my grandfather," she said.

The lieutenant looked her up and down, undressing her, imagining her laid out in the corpse's place.

"Your grandfather, you say? And what's your name?"

"My name is Fidelia, and this is my grandfather, Michael Angelos."

"And you've identified him just like that, Fidelia, from a distance?"

"It isn't me who says so, sir. It's my grandma. My grandma Sofia."

"Your grandma?"

"Yes, sir. My grandma."

"We know your grandmother all too well, Fidelia. And where might she be now? Would you know that?"

During the exchange of words, the girl was moving slowly and calmly toward the body. When she was by its side she sat down on a veined rock, her brown legs pressed together, and shaking out her hair, she took hold of one of the dead man's hard broken hands. Then she looked at the lieutenant with the full clarity of her eyes.

"She's with the captain again, sir. She went to ask permission to bury her husband the way he deserves."

⸗ iii ⸗

Toward nightfall, the captain, accompanied by and conversing with his orderly, will direct his steps toward the town church. By that time the heat will have eased a bit, a rustling blend of sounds will be rising from the alleyways, various neighbors will be coming out for a little fresh air. Even so, the captain will feel the heaviness of his feet, the years of fatigue collected in his thighs and his shoulders and back as he arrives to knock on the door of the priest's house. The priest himself will open the door.

"Good evening, Captain," he'll say in a somber and serious voice, unsurprised. "Come in, please."

You have to be careful with that one, Gheorghakis had advised him as soon as they were alone. He tends to protect antisocial elements, although he'd never admit it in public. And he's so well respected for his simplicity and poverty... We'd be crazy to pit ourselves against him. He has to be made to cooperate.

Gheorghakis wouldn't suggest that the captain cultivate his friendship, wouldn't go that far. Men of action have little to do with his sort. But every so often it wouldn't be a bad idea...attend mass in his church instead of with the chaplain of the regiment. These goddamned public relations...

But since then the captain had scarcely exchanged two or three sentences with Father Gabriel in passing or when they found themselves together in some house or on some street corner.

To the lieutenant, the visit had seemed unwise, a sign of weakness. That same afternoon he'd said so, just like that.

"My instructions are clear, Lieutenant," the captain replied. "To avoid incidents when possible... If we can straighten this problem out in the new spirit of national reconciliation... What'll you have?"

"Whiskey and water with plenty of ice, thank you, Captain."

"I want to see if this Father Gabriel is disposed to calm things down a little, that's all," the captain added, picking out the largest cubes and dropping them in the glass. "It's not that I lack the experience in this sort of thing. After all, I've just been in command of a regiment in a place where—"

"We all know what you're capable of, Captain. I'd never allow myself to doubt your resolution."

When the captain turned to examine the face that spoke these words, he found not the slightest hint of ridicule, no trace of anything suspicious. Now was the moment to keep quiet, to accept the unexpected praise. It was the moment to let his actions speak for themselves, proclaim the toughness of which he was no doubt capable. But he surprised himself by saying, "If Gheorghakis himself were here today, he'd be grinning at some dumb shopkeeper, going out to talk with the peasants to see if the harvests are due on time, inspecting the jails to see if they've been washed down twice a week." The lieutenant took his glass, tinkling the ice appreciatively. In this town, out in the middle of nowhere, it was a real luxury. The sound rang deliciously in the hot, thick air. But he made no comment, leaned neither for nor against this vision of a paternal, benevolent Gheorghakis.

The captain chewed back his desire to ask whether they still called Gheorghakis "the beast"—that's what they called him at the academy. And him, what would they call him? What sort of nickname did soldiers and subordinates whisper from regiment to regiment? Would he ever know?

"Perhaps, Captain, before making any decision, or in any case before visiting the priest, you should ascertain all the details first." The lieutenant nodded in the sergeant's direction. "I think we should hear the sergeant's report...."

But the captain will go to see the priest anyway. He'll be disgusted by the smell of old clothes, closed rooms, cheap food cooking, dusty books. That mild face too, of the man inviting him to have a seat, those cheeks excessively soft and pink, those fleshy lips, those hands so patient and vulnerable. He'll have a sudden crazy urge to slug that face, a lonesome, howling urge rising out of his guts ready to erupt and smash such a meek, peaceful face. What a pleasure it would be to finish things off once and for all.

"And to what do I owe the honor of this visit?" the priest will say, as the captain eases himself into the best seat in the house.

"I'm a man of few words, Father Gabriel," the captain will begin, "so I won't take much of your time."

The response will be obvious. The other has all the time the captain may need, there's no need to hurry.

"Father Gabriel. You know, and I know, that Longa is not the natural place to have a military post of this size. We know what accounts for such a situation: its proximity to these mountains"—and, inevitably, the captain will wave his hand toward the outside, although by this time darkness blocks the view of that steep nearby range, and there's an increasing sensation that everything inside here is even darker than out there, that the windows haven't been washed in a long time, that the only light is from this candelabrum on the table between the two—"these very mountains, where a center of subversion has been created which it hasn't been possible to eliminate without a more prolonged and direct course of action. It's my desire, and I assume yours and that of the whole population, to see the situation quickly changed, so that I, and the soldiers in my command, may leave this place as soon as possible."

There's too much understanding in the priest's eyes. He'll be taking in not just the words but their subterranean emotion. The captain will feel another sudden urge, this time to assure him that what he's saying is absolutely true, for months the only thing most of them have wanted is to go back home, he hasn't seen his family in so long he can't remember the faces of his children whose place has been taken by a photo he never shows anyone, as soon as possible is the plain truth. But why should Father Gabriel have any reason to believe what the lieutenant wouldn't understand. And anyway, one's sentiments don't count in such matters. So it's better just to continue. "That's the reason for my being here, and for the transfer of Captain Gheorghakis. I've come to initiate a process of normalization whose end result should be our departure before long."

"And Captain Gheorghakis?"

"He's carrying out an identical mission in another part of the country."

"Ah," the priest will say.

The captain will ignore this. His eyes will be fixed on the Christ that's moving and shaking in the dancing light of the candle flames. Then: "I assume you agree with me that this is best for everyone, not only for the region but the province and the country as well."

"Captain, whatever brings peace back to us," the priest will say, "can count on my most definite support."

"I'm glad you feel that way. Perhaps you can help us."

The priest does nothing more than fold his hands and nod his head, once. Whatever he might do, within his humble abilities.

"It's about that woman, Sofia Angelos. I don't know if you're aware of her recent...her recent..."

"Activities?"

"Yes, let's put it that way. Her recent activities."

Because what that old woman had done was go camp with her whole family beside the newest body, the body she'd claimed as her husband's. She was not the sort to stay quiet, trying to win the authorities over with a false obsequiousness. She meant business....

The captain had finished mixing his own drink and, sitting down on the edge of his desk, had signaled to the sergeant. "All the details?... Let's see that report, Sergeant."

"With your permission, Lieutenant."

The lieutenant had raised his glass, as if saying cheers and, at the same time, go ahead, Sergeant, proceed.

"When I arrived to carry out your orders, Captain, that is, to take the body and give it a Christian burial, I found them at the site. It's a fairly large family. Some eleven persons in all. In addition, the lady had brought five goats of hers to the spot. And two dogs."

"What you might call a family picnic," the captain commented, winking at the lieutenant, who raised his glass again, this time without bringing it to his lips.

"Yes, sir. Under some nearby trees they've improvised a table with a little tablecloth. It's actually some big rocks, and they had some fruit cooling in the river. They seemed to be preparing a fire, apparently for soup, Captain."

"Do they plan on spending the night? The whole night? Without men?"

"When I explained my mission to them in a deferential and respectful manner, as were my orders, the lady advised me that she wouldn't permit anyone but herself to bury her husband, that they had done it to her father against her wishes, but now her will would be done. She said neither she nor her family would move from the spot until the authorities granted her what she called her legitimate right."

The captain passed his drink from one hand to the other, then briefly sipped at it without taking his eyes off the florid face of the sergeant.

"And the family, are they all women?"

"No, Captain. Of the ten or eleven, two are boys. One about fourteen, maybe fifteen, and another smaller one, only about a year old, maybe a little more, it's hard to tell."

"A boy about fourteen, maybe fifteen," repeated the lieutenant, speaking for the first time in a long while. "The man of the family, eh?"

"You know him, Lieutenant?"

"Not yet, Captain, not yet. But he must be the oldest grandson of this nice lady. The cousin, perhaps the brother of the girl I told you about."

"Fidelia," said the sergeant.

"Fidelia," grinned the lieutenant.

"And who else is wandering around out there? What other persons have joined the group?"

"Without exactly forming part of the group, Captain, near it but not exactly part of it, one finds, at a certain distance, a few women. It's my impression that they come in rotation. There's always one or another, washing clothes, as far as I can figure. It's an impression, that's all."

"Three, four women from other families, taking turns. So we're well organized."

The captain got up from the table and finished off his drink. He gestured toward the orderly, who had stayed by the door all this time, as if he had his mind on something else or wasn't there at all. "And you, what do you think of this?"

The orderly answered at once, with a surprising fluency. "If you'll permit me, Captain, the situation is getting touchy. That woman is a professional agitator. The people around here are like animals when things get this way. All they think about is how to stir things up. They're not happy unless they're squabbling and fighting. And this lady's more of a troublemaker than the rest. It's just like the other body. She hadn't even seen it and she was already declaring to the four winds that it was her husband. Which is impossible, first of all because Michael Angelos isn't dead, second because nobody could ever positively identify a body in that state, and third because, in this case, as in the other, the ages just don't match up."

"Captain!"

The captain saw the rage rising in the lieutenant's face and raised a hand. "Easy, easy, let's have another little whiskey and take things slow."

"Captain," the lieutenant said again, "I think it's a conspiracy. I'm convinced that what we're faced with is a conspiracy."

And those words of the lieutenant's, detached from their rage and urgency, those same words will be the ones the captain will use later, at nightfall, in the priest's house....

"Activities?" the captain will say. "I suppose they could be called that. To us what's happening seems a bit more serious, Father Gabriel. We prefer to call things by their name. We prefer to say that we find ourselves facing a conspiracy."

The priest will watch his words carefully. It will be apparent that he has them under control, each one vaccinated as it appears. "It seems to me unjust to put things quite that way."

"Then how would you put them?"

"I consider it unfortunate that a woman of that age and responsibility should see herself forced to carry out such an action."

"Forced? Are you justifying her attitude?"

"It's not my place to judge humankind, sir. That's not our privilege. I simply observe that she, like many other women in this area, is suffering an inhuman situation, and that's where one must seek out the source of such desperate acts, acts that have no chance of succeeding."

At this point the captain will show himself to be truly perplexed. "You really believe they're senseless, purely desperate acts?" he asks. "How interesting. You really believe that?"

"I didn't say senseless, Captain. That's your word. The real situation couldn't be more extreme, and that's what I'm referring to. Sofia Angelos wants a funeral for someone she considers her next of kin. The army won't allow it."

"Considers her next of kin? And you, what do you think? Could it really be her husband?"

The priest's lips will tremble. For a magnificent instant the captain will feel he has him cornered. He'll note the uneasiness, the doubt. He'll see it in the way the priest wants to get up but finally stays seated facing him.

The priest sighs. "To tell the truth, Captain, no, I consider it very unlikely." And since the captain won't let a triumphant smile slip onto his face, since he remains calm and unruffled even if he is hearing from the women's defender the same arguments that he himself or the sergeant or the lieutenant have exchanged all afternoon, since the captain keeps quiet, the priest will feel encouraged to continue. "It's more than a matter of the basic data not seeming to correspond: age, build, as far as I can recall, and the rest. It's that it would certainly be strange for a body that's been in the water two or three days or perhaps a week to wash up in precisely the same town where it was born, where it had lived, and beyond that be recovered by kinfolk. As this has happened twice now, no, in reality it's very hard to believe. God has accustomed us to miracles, and He could be working in mysterious ways. But I've given you my opinion, Captain, confidentially of course."

"And I'm grateful for it, Father Gabriel." The captain will pull his chair up until his uniform bumps the table. He'll see how the candles cast flickering shadows against the wall, and in the silence he'll also feel the breath of the orderly at his back, the silky, panting, anxious attention of the orderly taking everything in, more like a hunchback, more like an idiot, a piece of furniture, a filthy-minded sentry, the shadows raking strange figures across the wall. "So you wouldn't perform funeral services under that name? Answer me that, man to man."

The priest will focus on his fine soft hands playing with the candelabrum before answering.

"It's a puzzling situation, yes, puzzling, because in my heart of hearts I still have doubts about the true identity of the deceased. But since you ask, since you put it that way, man to man, all right, I'll answer yes, that if she came to ask my help, I'd perform the funeral rites."

For just an instant, without knowing why or where the sensation comes from, the captain will feel his head swimming with the idea that it's not the orderly behind him but the lieutenant. He'll hold back the absurd impulse to turn around and see who's actually there, watching him, registering every word he says, and furiously, so both men can hear him, he'll spit out, "Even though you feel you're dealing with a fraud, a trick, a mockery of God!"

"Strong words, Captain," the priest will say smoothly. "Words you haven't carefully considered. For reasons of your own which I have no right to examine. I'm not going to ask you to retract them, Captain. Instead, I'll ask you a question. Let's ask ourselves who killed that man, how he died, how he ended up in the river."

"Dead from accidental causes," the captain will say, an uneasy note in his voice, as he studies the feminine, rosy, almost pleasant cheeks of the priest, and that benign hand again carefully straightening the candelabrum. "That's what the doctor determined, that's what the judge in the district capital will confirm tomorrow or the next day."

"I've just shown a certain trust in you as a person, Captain, admitting doubts as to the identity of the dead man which I would never confess in public. Let's see if you'll show the same trust in me."

"All right, let's see."

"Do you have the slightest, the faintest shadow of a doubt that that man was brutally mistreated before he died, the same as the first corpse that came floating down the river about two weeks ago? Might there not be a systematic campaign to intimidate the population, to make them understand that many of their men are hostages and that the best thing they can do is to cooperate with the authorities? Or do you have some other explanation for these events?"

The captain will respond with excessive speed, rising from his seat, biting off each hot word. "And do you believe"—the captain will hear his voice saying with a passion hardly called for by the question—"it's to our advantage that nameless, faceless corpses should wash up from the river every two weeks? Do you think that the government, which is doing everything it can to limit the presence of foreign troops now occupying part of our territory, would be acting in such a way? Do you think we don't have other methods of disposing of bodies than dumping them stupidly in rivers so that later they'll explode in our face like a ton of dynamite? Do you think I approve of this kind of situation just when I have instructions to proceed benevolently, to open a new and peaceful phase in our relations with the rebels? You want to know something? I'm tired of this war too. We want it to end. For everyone's sake."

"I believe you, Captain, but it's really very simple to end all this. And you know it. Release the political prisoners. The known ones and also the secret ones, the ones you have hidden out there. The day that Mrs. Angelos's father comes back, and her husband, and her sons, and those of all these other poor women, that day you can bury whatever body turns up in the river however you please. And I wager you, that day no more corpses will appear."

This time the captain won't reply right away. Because he's been thinking the same sort of thing himself, that very afternoon when the lieutenant denounced the conspiracy, that very moment when a second body lay on the beach, that first time he'd seen the old woman outside his door, motionless, waiting for him, and something like that also when he'd received his new instructions, the plan of national reconciliation, the amnesty, the ferocious reports of Captain Gheorghakis. But on this he won't take the priest into his confidence, just as he didn't let the lieutenant in on his thoughts. On the contrary, he'd simply nodded affirmatively....

"I believe it's a conspiracy too, Lieutenant. But what they want us to do, precisely, is to act too hastily. What could be better for them than if we attacked a family of women and children in order to take possession of a corpse? What better present for our enemies? Yesterday I would have given a peremptory order to clear the site and bury the body without thinking twice."

"I don't doubt it, Captain."

"Tomorrow perhaps I'll have the pleasure of giving that order again."

"It's very likely, Captain."

"But today? Today we have to proceed calmly and shrewdly, disarming our adversaries, foiling their plans. And above all, avoiding an intervention by German troops, don't you think so? Because the day we set about repressing women and children, that's a sign we no longer control the territory under our command, correct?"

The lieutenant set his glass down on the desk. "I couldn't agree with you more, Captain. I confess my only fear is that the situation may really become unstable again, and then we'll have to act with greater force for not having intervened when we could have nipped the trouble in the bud."

"We'll nip it in the bud, Lieutenant, we'll give it a good nip."

"As long as another body doesn't appear, Captain."

"Another body?" The captain took out his cigarette case, offered the lieutenant a cigarette, remembered he didn't smoke, and lit one for himself. "Tell me, Lieutenant. Who do you think—exactly who—is throwing these little bodies in the river?"

"As we've been given no official interpretation, Captain, I prefer to offer no opinion. The only thing I'm sure of, sir, is that there's a conspiracy going on. They lost the shooting war. Now they're trying to win some other way, taking advantage of our outstretched hand."

"In war, Lieutenant, sometimes one crushes the enemy and sometimes one gives him the chance to surrender. That's the way war is."

Just then the captain had noticed the orderly observing from the doorway, absorbing every word into some slippery cranny of his memory, and he'll remember him again that night, standing invisible behind his back, listening in on the conversation with the priest like some goddamned sponge, because the captain will also speak of war then, he'll have to respond by speaking of war....

"Father Gabriel," the captain will say, "this is a war. There are dead on both sides. I also lost a brother, a cousin. There are winners and losers. That's how wars are. Now we're putting an end to this one. Because we have the strength to impose peace. It would be better if you, instead of preaching retribution, would ask the faithful to forgive and forget."

"War, Captain..."

And again the captain will feel a surge of hatred for the priest's deep, cowlike eyes, the tenderness gathered in that sensual mouth, the motions of a hand accustomed to turning pages and to solitary nights, the almost feminine, almost exquisite eyelashes.

"The laws of war. Then return the dead to their families. If her husband Michael died out there, doesn't it seem more Christian to inform her of that, so that she might accept it and face it like a real widow and not a...half widow? More Christian and more political as well."

"Better leave politics to us military men, and you tend to matters of the soul."

"That's what I'm tending to, Captain, precisely that."

Then the captain will rise from his seat, and this time the contained violence of his impulse will knock the chair backwards, the orderly catching it before it hits the floor.

"All right," the captain will say, "it's clear I have no alternative but to act without your cooperation," without yet having told the priest what he's come for, what sort of help he was going to request.

"I never declined to cooperate. You asked my opinion, I'm giving it to you. If I can intervene to bring spirits into agreement, to arrange a dialogue between the parties so as to avoid any incidents we would all regret later..."

"But you wouldn't be willing to go to the river and convince this Angelos woman to give up her rebellious attitude? To explain to her that there's no chance whatever of our yielding on this point, and that what I can offer, on my word of honor, is to have for her within a reasonable time—say four to six months—more precise information concerning the disappearance of her husband?"

"You're offering her information about a man she believes is right there beside her, dead. I doubt if she'll accept. I can try, of course."

"And in addition," the captain will say, sensing that now is the time to show his cards, that everything's falling into place according to plan, "we would release the boy, Alexis."

"Alexis? You're holding Alexis prisoner?"

...Yes, they were holding him prisoner. Because that's the way war is, the captain had explained to the lieutenant. You strike and you negotiate. The captain's orders had been peremptory.

"Sergeant, you're going to double the guard down there. I don't want too large a force, it shouldn't be a case where they say we've surrounded a seemingly innocent group, but the presence of the army—discreet yet definite—should be felt. Stop every woman who comes or goes from the scene, take their names, question them on every kind of thing: reasons for having visited those people, identity and occupations of the men in the family, suggestions that their washing can be done upriver, etc. Understood?"

"Yes, Captain. Anything else, Captain?"

The captain had felt the colorless piercing eyes of the lieutenant boring into him but neither returned the look nor allowed the slightest wavering in his voice.

"And bring me that kid. I want to talk to him alone. Let's see if we understand each other man to man...."

His reply to the priest will be equally certain, polished, conclusive. "It's my opinion, Father Gabriel, that we're faced with a conspiracy of as yet unknown dimensions. We didn't throw those bodies into this or any other river. Someone is trying to create a situation where we see ourselves forced to crack down. Someone wants to obstruct, sabotage, or twist the efforts the Supreme Government has begun to make toward reconciliation. They want to take advantage of the painful situation of a few families in order to provoke another escalation of violence. I'm sure I don't need to remind you it was due to that violence that foreign troops massively entered the country in the first place. A renewal of it could increase their number instead of leading to their eventual withdrawal. I want you to know, Father, that this case can't be isolated from other incidents that are shaking the country."

"And what does the boy have to do with all this?"

"That's what we're trying to determine, Father, what the boy has to do with all this, the national and international ramifications of this movement. He's the only man in that family. You know it's useless trying to talk to the females. These or any others. But especially these. You know them better than I do."

"It doesn't make sense to do anything to Alexis. That boy wouldn't hurt a lizard."

"So far I've been patient in my actions, very patient. If I wait another day, people are going to think, and word's going to get around, that we've lost our grip on things, that it's time to put on pants and act like men. And believe me, Father Gabriel, I'm the one who's wearing the pants around here."

The captain will note the priest's round shoulders, his weariness, his cheeks drained of their innocence, his beautiful old defeated eyes, his mouth a little weaker all the time.

"So what is it exactly that you want me to do, Captain?"

Because the moment will have come for the captain to explain what he expects of him, what he has in mind....

The priest doesn't know, has no way of knowing, that the captain has spoken with the orderly. On the way to the church, in the dusk that scarcely relieved the heat, in the same dense dust that was always swirling slowly in the air, they had scarcely left headquarters, scarcely found themselves alone, there, then, at that moment.

The orderly's voice was hoarse.

"If you'll permit me, Captain."

"I'm listening." The captain took off, walking up the street.

"With your permission, Captain, something you said gave me an idea. Maybe it could help clear up...the situation."

The captain stopped. "Fine," he said, trying to regain a little good humor after the conversation with the lieutenant. "We're about to speak with a man of God, so I'm going to answer you as he would. Any idea that may contribute to the cause of peace should be carefully considered. So go ahead."

"I was thinking about that old woman's father, Karoulos Mylonas, Captain."

"Her father?"

"Excuse me, Captain, I mean the man she said was her father, the first dead man."

"Ah, that one."

"Yes, sir. I was thinking that if you consented, it's a sort of strange idea, sir, if you consented to that woman's first request, as far as returning the body and allowing a funeral, private, of course, and not too big, if you let her go ahead with that, on condition that she immediately leave the scene in question, well, I thought that perhaps that might be a way out of the...the tangle, Captain."

"Trading her the so-called father for the so-called husband," the captain muttered. "It's crazy. They never prepared us for this sort of thing at the academy. A small funeral, strictly private, this very night, without informing anyone beyond the immediate family."

"Yes, Captain."

"Could be. Could be. Let's ask our friend Father Gabriel how this possibility looks to him. Let's pop it at the end of the conversation after we've softened him up a bit, see if he'll cooperate with us then."

"Whatever you say, sir."

They went on in silence to the priest's house. The captain knocked. But before anyone answered, he turned toward the orderly and threw out one last doubt.

"Just a minute. And this new body. What do we do with it? Because as soon as they get the first one buried they'll want to get their hands on the second."

"Not necessarily, sir," the orderly had answered hurriedly. "That can also be taken care of."

Just then the door swung open. It was the priest himself.

"Good evening, Captain," he said. His voice was somber and serious, unsurprised. "Come in, please."

They went in.

chapter two

⸾ iv ⸾

Something was going to happen. All the women knew that much, since the day of the funeral we had known it, since the day Fidelia had seen her brother's face between the two soldiers and Mama had squeezed her hand. Mama squeezed my hand even harder when they brought Alexis back, but she didn't ask my brother a thing, didn't want to ask him. Since that moment, since then all of us had known. Just leave a pot boiling till it boils over and then pour more water in and try to force the lid down and anybody knows what can, what has to happen.

There were Mama's shoulders, a heap of stones piling up on Mama's back; we women watched Alexandra's shoulders like people coming out of a house to check a cloudy sky with the wind building and trying to figure out when the storm will break. We saw her surround herself like a castle with such huge walls that it ends up being nothing but walls. We saw her deliberately, proudly letting the seconds go by before answering one of Grandma's simplest questions. I knew Mama: when she shut her lips together like that, when they went white with the pressure, you had to be careful, because deep inside her the heart was on the point of lashing out like a trapped cat. Mama had always been that way, even when Papa was here, her rage would build for days until it was ready to... But Papa knew how to disarm her; Dimitriou would take her by the waist and start spinning her around, dancing with her, singing out loud, pretending he was doing a radio interview trying to get at why she was so upset, and he'd call her his hot pepper, his magic powder keg, my dynamite, beguiling witch and guiding star, sweet hurricane and other dumb stuff, and Alexis and I would laugh and finally Mama too. Nobody could stay sad or mad with Dimitriou there; Papa was so crazy he was beautiful. But who could prevent what was happening now? Me?

Alexis? Any of us women? And the worst thing was that we all knew it, every one of us, except Grandma. She just went right on, preferring to take no part in the fear and rage brewing between Mama's legs, and Mama not knowing what to do with her feelings, dead birds I thought in spite of myself I thought of dead birds trying to fly that couldn't get out of Mama's eyes, the hot rain of her body building up between her legs, getting ready, getting ready. Grandma was the only one who didn't want to acknowledge those words that Alexandra was biting back, and I remembered when I was little making up a story to scare Alexis about how Mama had a hungry wolf inside her that fed on her blood, a wolf that would have to come out one day because his feasts wouldn't be enough for him and this wolf obeyed only me so Alexis had better be careful, but then I began to believe it myself, Fidelia herself got scared. Only now we knew what was filling Alexandra so steadily, silently; we knew it was Dimitriou. It was Papa's absence howling around inside her when they brought back Alexis and I couldn't look in his eyes and Mama squeezed my hand until it hurt, both my hands hurt, I knew it wouldn't be long, that something was going to explode.

As soon as we saw her come back from the market that day, we knew the time had come. It was a matter of noticing how she stopped at the edge of the patio, like a stranger troubling us for some water or delivering a letter with bad news. Fidelia told us later that she'd wanted to intervene, distract Mama's attention with some kind of foolishness, but before she could do it Alexis shook his head no, it wouldn't work, and it was better not to get up or do anything, if he couldn't change her intentions what was I going to accomplish? No one in the world was going to stop her now, only the sudden blessing of Papa's appearance, that kind of miracle, and the only thing left was to keep on, like all the women, working as if we didn't know what she was going to say, as if we could erase her words before they were pronounced or put off for a few more centuries what was happening right in front of our eyes, Alexandra and Grandma face to face, Grandma and Mama tangled up in one another like shipwrecks in a storm, without being able later to rein in what one of them had let loose who knows how, because Alexandra believed, and she shot it out just like that, all at once, right there at home, on the patio, at the door of the house, the house that belonged to all of us, in front of the whole family and in front of Fidelia and in front of Alexis who shouldn't have had to witness the spats of women, Alexandra said it just like that, without talking it over in private as some of us might have hoped, the way it's always been done between mother-in-law and daughter-in-law in a family like ours, and she gave no warning, it just jumped out of her mouth like a black, drunken spider that had been languishing between her teeth all these weeks, said she believed that they, that we, and I could foresee the discussion and the silence and the recriminations again and again for days and weeks, maybe months, everything that was going to start right now and no one could stop it, she believed that Grandma—

"We're killing our own men, Grandma," Alexandra said. "You're killing them."

And she pronounced the word *Grandma* as one pronounces the words *old woman*. Like that.

We all thought, now, yes, here it comes. But Grandma didn't even look at Alexandra. She kept on grinding wheat in the stone mortar, pulling out the stone with a catlike quickness and letting it slide back in, moving her hands peacefully in the process. Is that so? And how much did you get for the milk, girl? More than last week? Give Alexis the money, please. Let's see if soon we don't have enough for another trip to the capital, we're not going to keep selling goats, maybe now that scoundrel of a judge would hear us out.

But Mama wasn't ready for a truce. We all could tell she wouldn't accept this or any absolution. She wanted to thrash things out right now, not later, when the rest of us women wouldn't be here and

Alexis gone. Alexandra raised her voice so that there wouldn't be another chance for useless reconciliation. Our own men, Grandma, a mistake was being made, a mistake that the whole community would end up paying for, and the family too, and what's more, she wasn't the only one who thought so.

Grandma set about examining the money my brother had collected. She counted it ever so slowly. We watched each coin fall from one palm to the other. Then she asked Alexis if he'd be good enough to note the amount and place the money in the box on top of the table. Did he know which box she meant? Gently reminding us, making Alexandra remember that beside the box stood the photos of the men of the family, our men, and among them the one of Papa, of Dimitriou.

Alexis wasn't sure. We could tell by the way he blinked his eyes. This was Alexandra's job. It was Mama who kept accounts, who knew how to get the best prices at the market, was famous for how fast she could multiply and subtract; better than me, Father Gabriel would say, moving his head with sadness and admiration; if your mother had only been able to stay in school. Grandma placed the coins in his hand and closed his fingers around them and repeated, Go ahead, Alexis, that his Mama wouldn't have time today for that, there was a lot to talk about, and right away, as if Alexis were already headed into the house, she said to Alexandra that tomatoes never went up, it was impossible to figure how the sellers who came all the way from Alabakis could keep their prices so low, now there's a real conspiracy all right if the authorities were so eager to find one. Then we watched her going over the wheat with her expert, malicious eyes, her look a sieve that caught what wasn't quite fine enough.

Is that what Alexandra Orphanaxos thought? The menace in Grandma's voice was all the sharper because her tone stayed the same. She spat it out smoothly, almost the way she casually noted the sickness of the neighbors' baby or the lack of decent tea lately. Is that what she thought? And not only Alexandra Orphanaxos, wife of her oldest son, Dimitriou, but other women of Longa as well, with and without men, were they saying that? And perhaps in this family more than one thought the same thing? Someone else here agreed with Alexandra and walked around muttering privately what she wouldn't dare admit in public? Was that so?

And she swept her gaze back and forth over us all. It pierced each one of us, including me, she looked at Fidelia with distrust, even knowing she could always count on her granddaughter, that whenever anyone opposed her she could always be sure I'd be there, she was accusing even me of plotting behind her back. I had heard my aunts whispering what Mama had just announced out loud, but none of us answered. We went about our business as quietly as before, as if this had nothing to do with us. We were waiting for Alexandra to speak. Mama had opened the door, it was she who'd have to find a way to shut it.

But what Mama did was to speak to Alexis. He shouldn't take the money in yet, she'd do it later. This had to do with his father, it was right that he be present, he was a man now or had to pretend he was in times like these, God knows.

Alexis stood in the doorway, stopped there, at the threshold, waiting, not minding either one. He folded his arms like Papa would have and didn't say a word, leaning against the wall. He was a quiet boy, so this didn't surprise us. But he had been quieter than usual, had hardly opened his mouth since they let him go that night. We saw him appear between the two soldiers. It was past midnight when they finally kept their promise and took him out of the jail so he could attend the funeral, and since then he wouldn't talk, didn't say a thing. He put his shoulder under the coffin that we were already supporting, and started walking up the hill, without even looking at the lieutenant or the two soldiers, and didn't let out a syllable, not then or later, and none of us asked any questions either, not even Alexandra, not even Fidelia. We preferred not to know what had happened to him. We didn't want him to answer the questions we'd never ask.

Then I raised my eyes for as long as it takes a pigeon to fly over, and he was looking at me sitting among the other women spinning, and I was glad for that glancing visit of his coffee-colored eyes the same as mine and I smiled as I had when they brought him back that night, so he'd know I was there nearby, but the rest didn't break their rhythm for even a second. I had to go on with the work like the rest, just as the hill had to be climbed with great-grandfather's body. We concentrated on our spinning, almost imagining Alexandra and Grandma to be elsewhere, in some foreign country where snow was falling instead of the sun burning down so hard.

There was a moment of calm. I didn't want it to end. I wanted us to get up and make some lunch, or collect honey or wood for the fire or look after Serguei the baby, or I wished we were little kids again with Papa coming back from the country, one of us on each shoulder. I wanted to shut my eyes, to see if when I opened them up I could find Papa's face peeking out from behind the tree, like one of those bearded archangels in church, Papa rising up with big wings on his shoulders and laughing at them both, his mother and his wife, I'm going to spank you two, let them learn from my little love Fidelia not to make trouble, isn't that so my peach? I prayed that God would hear me, I promised him I'd never make any trouble if Papa would appear right now, take me away and bring him back, prayed that he would answer me with a father so that Mama'd have someone to lean on, so there'd be someone, there'd be someone.

Then Grandma spoke.

Killing them? A mistake? Hadn't the family managed to bury Karoulos Mylonas, her father, after that Gheorghakis denied it, after this new one, this so-called captain, counseled by that devil of a lieutenant, did the same? Hadn't they felt the satisfaction of fulfilling God's laws so the old man might rest in peace, with rites administered by a real priest? Hadn't they rescued him from the godless, pagan earth of the military, who only paid lip service to Christ, those soldiers your own husband Dimitriou always hated? She, she and her family, she had brought it about. With the help of everyone here, with the help of Hilda, her only living sister, with the help of her three daughters, with her own daughters-in-law, among them Alexandra, and even Fidelia, and Alexis, what about Alexis, she had managed to bend the hand and the will of that officer and his band of cutthroats. It was clear that this one was even more spineless than Gheorghakis, that he hadn't dared use force against a just cause and a defenseless woman. And did she know why? Because the whole population approved of what she'd done, the other women were ashamed of their own cowardice. Or could it be that Alexandra, not carrying the same blood in her veins, was incapable of understanding the importance of what she was accomplishing?

Maybe before coming out with such accusations again she ought to consider a few facts. The man they'd all buried this past Monday was Dimitriou's grandfather, father of these two creatures. Had she thought about that? Dimitriou wouldn't even have been born if the man they'd buried hadn't received Dimitriou's parents, her and her husband, offering them a place in this very house when there wasn't any work and Michael fell sick and had no father or mother himself, received them with open arms, even though there wasn't food in the pot for the ones already here. And if she didn't believe it she could ask Hilda, here present. That was the winter Dimitriou was born. And even if Alexandra had forgotten that act of kindness and all the other standards of parenthood, at least she ought to have the decency and the courtesy to watch her tongue, regardless of what she thought. She wasn't asking her to respect Dimitriou's mother, but Dimitriou himself, for whom she'd surely have to take the same action, and then they'd need to stick together, the whole family, whenever that day came.

There was a lull. Until then, Mama had chosen to stay out there, frozen at the edge of the tree's shadow, the sunlight falling across her shoulders and long hair, casting a terrible whitish glow over her as she punished herself with the heat, always at a distance, always apart. Suddenly, as though something had melted, she came to sit next to Grandma.

"Mama," said Alexandra, and that word said everything, "that's what I'm talking about, Mama, I don't want anything to happen to Dimitriou."

The anger vanished from her voice. In those two or three seconds some mysterious hidden angel had drained and dried out the swamp building up in her throat all this time. Grandma's words had been enough. They left no room for blind passions. Or maybe it was simply that for the first time in months she'd said what she feared, had had the courage to put Papa there, where we could all see him, to speak of her fear and relieve it because it was the same fear we all felt. That was Mama, just like Alexis and I could remember her, quiet and gentle and a little melancholy as she went on weaving because she didn't believe in too much happiness, just rocking herself alone. It was the Alexandra of an earlier time, bathed in the light rising out of two children about to be born, fixing breakfast for Dimitriou and the other men in the light of dawn, waiting for our men a little before sundown, a basket of fruit rocking in the wind. Her rage had burnt itself out and in its place she had that strange peace of rivers when they flow into a rough sea.

Grandma saw that. She stopped grinding the wheat and in the way she held the stone in the air she'd responded. She didn't want anything to happen to Dimitriou either, but there are some things, too many things we simply can't control, girl.

"Dimitriou's alive, Mama," said Alexandra. "I know he's alive. I know it in here."

Grandma looked at her, we all looked at her hand on her heart.

Grandma made a gesture as if to catch it, a cluster of grapes about to fall, but checked herself. She looked at Alexandra's hand as if some crows were carrying it off in the wind, she raised the stone and let it slide back toward the wheat.

"It's what we all want," said Grandma. "God knows."

"They're letting some prisoners go," said Hilda, suddenly. "Dimitriou could be one of them."

"And Serguei," said Cristina, looking at us, looking at Yanina. Grandma spoke up hoarsely, scornfully. Rumors like those had been circulating for months and none of the men who'd been taken away had ever appeared, not one. All that was left was to see that they had a decent funeral, a piece of ground to lie down in, a piece of sacred ground, and hope that the rest were alive and would return soon, to be patient until Alexis was bigger and could ask for explanations as a man. And if that captain was seen in the taverns promising that pretty soon some women would get a surprise, a big surprise, a surprise that was going to please some women, fine, that was the captain's business, that was that traitor of an orderly's business. There was no point in fooling ourselves. Now we had to collect our energies for another purpose. We had to get them to give us Michael Angelos's body. She had proved it was possible, she'd shown all those cowardly milkless women that faith is rewarded. There was the cross with her father's name. There on the hill was proof.

"Grandma," said Alexandra. "Grandma, enough death. Grandma, enough of this talk of death all day, nothing but the graveyard and death. Grandma, they're going to kill Dimitriou. They're going to kill him if we don't do something."

For a long time, nobody said a word. Fidelia went on spinning with a steady hand, I went on eyeing my hands as if they were some other girl's. I was thinking of Papa, wishing Grandma would just ask Mama once and for all, that someone would ask her what she had heard at the market, how could she be sure Papa was alive, how could she be sure he was going to be killed. But the only thing that happened was that little Serguei began to cry, on time as always, hungry as always. No one got up to look at him, not even Yanina, who waited with the rest of us while the silence became worse with the baby's cries, the silence that kept asking and asking the questions about Papa and all the men, and all of a sudden my own voice surprised me flying out of my insides like a bird escaping. It was strange that I couldn't hear the mad pounding of my heart in my voice, it felt like it was trying to jump out of me, strange that no one could hear Papa's presence, Papa's absence, covering everything, beating in my voice.

"Mama," Fidelia said, still working, not raising her eyes to Alexandra. "Mama, isn't it time to tell us what happened today? Did you hear anything at the market, Mama?"

She came over to me and took my hands off the loom and held them between hers. When she answered she did it slowly, with difficulty, each word hurting her, not wanting to say what she had to.

"There's someone else who's claiming the body, Fidelia," Mama whispered. "That's what's happening. They're never going to give us that body."

"Someone else?" Grandma stopped suddenly and the wheat fell and we saw the mortar roll at her feet. She didn't make the least attempt to pick anything up. "What did you say? Someone else?"

The dropping of the mortar and the spilled wheat seemed a prearranged signal: we all stopped working for the first time since Alexandra had arrived, waiting for the answer. But it wasn't she who spoke.

It was my brother.

Without moving from his place by the door, with his arms still folded, but no longer leaning against the wall, he said the first words we'd heard him say since they'd put him in jail.

"Sarakis," Alexis said, as if that explained everything. "That woman Sarakis is going to claim Grandpa's body. She says it's the body of her brother Theodoro. The captain's going to give him to her and she's going to rebury him."

"That whore?" Grandma turned her body toward Alexis without moving her feet which were planted in the same place like two tense trembling roots, while she stretched her whole body toward him, her arms in the air. "That whore's going to claim my husband's body? She dares to use Theodoro? Her own brother? Theodoro who hated them, who cursed them in front of everyone as traitors, who'd kick them if he came back, kick them, her and her slut of a daughter and the orderly too. They're going to use our friend Theodoro for that? To take my husband away from me? That whore?"

"Yes," said Alexis. "That one."

Grandma bent to pick up the mortar and then sat down again on the bench, her shoulders were weighing her down. "Now what will we do?" she whispered, trying to keep the hysteria out of her voice, speaking almost to herself, her arms broken branches hanging down. "The captain will do it, the captain will give my Michael to that witch. He's going to give him to her. If only Theodoro were here. Theodoro would kick her into line right in the street, her and that whore Cecilia and that orderly fag. Like when they were young, with Michael. Nobody could stop those two. Theodoro would know what to do. If we could ask him, he'd know what to do."

"Our friend Theodoro isn't coming back, Grandma," said Alexis. "It's two years since they took him, and if they're using him for that, it's because they know he's never coming back."

"Never?" Grandma asked. "Theodoro's never coming back? But then what will we do? What on earth can we do?"

I felt Mama letting my hands go all of a sudden and I wanted to hold hers just a little longer but they'd already gone.

"Never?" Alexandra said hoarsely, addressing Grandma or maybe no one. "He's never going to come back?"

Then for the second time that day Fidelia uttered the words we were all waiting for, we saw her adolescent frame step forward.

"Alexis," I said to my brother, quietly, like someone setting a table, almost indifferent. "Alexis, what'll we do?"

With two vigorous strides, Alexis stepped out to the center of the patio, next to his mother and grandmother, who looked at him like they'd never seen him before. None of us could believe that he had once cried like Serguei was crying now, yesterday he and Fidelia sleeping in the same bed where the baby was now, calling to us for attention.

Suddenly, over the cries from the house for some hand of some grown, comforting mother, Yanina not moving as was her duty, over those cries Alexis spoke, stressing every word so we'd hear.

"Either he belongs to us all or he belongs to nobody. All the women have to claim him for burial, all the families."

"And then?"

Who asked that? Me, us, Grandma, Alexandra, who asked?

"And then," Alexis answered carefully, with Dimitriou's voice now, it was Papa's own tough and tender and pregnant voice, "and then we'll see."

chapter three

⸿ V ⸿

"Next," said the judge. "I hope I get a good lunch after all this torture."

"Longa takes pride in its roast lamb with mint," the captain said cheerfully. "And we've put a few little bottles of white wine on ice to help you forget your troubles."

"That lamb will have to be awfully good, and the nap afterward nice and deep, Captain, to make up for this. A fifteen-hour trip from Alabakis—I've been through worse, of course, but ten of these women, Captain, ten, just this morning, when one is enough to drive you crazy."

"Console yourself with the thought there are only twenty-seven more."

"Or better yet," added the lieutenant, "that we have to deal with them every day of the year, twenty-four hours a day, while you can devote yourself to more useful and entertaining matters."

"And you haven't even had to face old Sofia."

"Now at least we know why all these guys are missing"—it was the lieutenant again—"with such impossible hags to put up with..."

"All right, all right, I give up," said the judge. "You're heroes, you deserve medals. The next one, bring on the next one."

"It's Katherina Theogonafis," announced the orderly from the doorway, and the judge's clerk checked the name on his list as the woman made her appearance.

"Good morning," said the judge. "You may be seated."

Katherina Theogonafis arranged herself on the edge of the chair and nervously eyed the four men seated behind the captain's desk.

"Clerk, kindly inform us, in brief, of the nature of the request."

"That's not necessary, Your Honor, I already know what I want and so do you, same as the captain and the lieutenant."

"It's a matter of legal procedure, woman," the captain said. "Better keep quiet and answer only when you're spoken to."

She didn't reply.

Rising, the clerk began to read the petition in question, wherein Mrs. Katherina Theogonafis affirmed her right and her obligation to bury her deceased husband, the former mayor Mr. Andrei Theogonafis, who had been found dead on Monday, June 8, as she was doing her washing alongside other women, dead of undetermined although accidental causes, added the clerk in a bored flat tone, and that she had drawn up this petition in light of the fact that the nation's army had taken charge of the body, burying it in some unknown location. For these reasons, she would be most pleased to be granted permission to fulfill her duties as wife and mother of the children of the deceased, giving him a funeral as he deserved. She was accompanied by the proper official documents, a document of baptism, a certificate of marriage by the church, and the baptism documents of the six children begotten by her and Mr. Andrei Theogonafis.

"Very well," said the judge. "Now we all know what you want. Now perhaps you could answer a couple of insignificant questions. Let's say there are still some doubts about this whole affair, wouldn't you agree?"

"As you wish, sir."

"Let's see. When did you know that the man who appeared that Monday, June 8, was your husband?"

"Sir?"

"The judge is asking you," explained the lieutenant, biting off each word, "if you knew it was your husband right away, that morning when he was found by the river."

"Yes, sir. I suspected it immediately."

"You suspected it?" The judge removed his glasses and wiped them with a handkerchief. "It was just a suspicion?"

"It's the first thing one thinks, sir, when one has a husband far away, sir. With your permission, one's thoughts grow dark and as soon as you hear of some mishap, well, you imagine that it has to do with the loved one."

"So that's why you thought immediately that this was the former mayor, Mr. Andrei Theogonafis, your husband?"

"Yes, sir. Something leaped in my heart and I said to myself, That's him, they killed him. Don't you see, we were all affected by the case of Karoulos Mylonas, who we'd found in the river a while before. So we always went down to the river to do our washing a little early and we all thought perhaps we'd find some relative. Don't you see how many we're missing? Life is very hard for the smaller children like this, sir."

"But you didn't identify him immediately?"

"Yes, sir, immediately."

The lieutenant made a gesture with his hand to the judge. "That's a lie. You told me, in the presence of the regiment's doctor and four soldiers and several other witnesses, that you had not the slightest idea as to the dead man's identity. And now you inform us that you identified him. Withholding information from the authorities, madam, is a crime in our penal code. Did you know that?"

"I identified him, but I wasn't going to tell you, Lieutenant, sir. Who knows what would have been done to me if I told you?"

"What would have been done to you? What would have been done to you?" groaned the captain. "He would have been given to you for burial, Mrs. Theogonafis, that's what the lieutenant would have done, and you would have saved us all these problems now."

The woman calmly folded her hands. "That's what you say now, Captain, sir. But then things were different. Why did Captain Gheorghakis deny Sofia Angelos the right to bury her own father, may he rest in peace, and now she's been allowed to do it?"

"Please, gentlemen. We shouldn't let ourselves get worked up.

We're here to investigate the circumstances surrounding a petition by this woman and thirty-six others concerning a dead man called for the time being N. N. Let's proceed. How did you know, madam, that this was your husband?"

"I knew it as soon as we pulled him out of the water, sir, may God forgive me. As we were bringing him ashore and I touched him, well, sir, one knows these things, after twenty-nine years of marriage. Last May it would have been thirty, poor soul, one isn't going to make mistakes about something like that."

"And you didn't think you were committing a very grave sin and an eternal transgression, letting your husband be taken away and buried in some common grave, while you did nothing?"

"Yes, sir, I felt I was condemning myself, sir. That's why I've brought up this petition that the clerk has there, to correct the error, because I couldn't get any sleep that night and I know that if I don't give him a proper burial I'll have to regret it forever and my children will blame me and his mother would too if she were alive."

"And what did you think when the girl Fidelia said that the body was that of her grandfather Michael?"

"What did I think, do you want to know?"

"Yes, what did you think when that girl claimed for her family the body which you believe to be that of your own husband?"

"I thought Sofia had made a mistake. She hadn't yet come to see the corpse, so how was she going to know if it was Michael?"

"Exactly," shouted the captain. "That's exactly what I said. She had come straight here, as soon as she knew of the body, isn't that right, Sergeant?"

"Yes, sir, that's how it was."

"And I also thought," Katherina went on, "that a family couldn't accumulate two dead men, I mean it was too much bad luck for Sofia to be faced with her husband's body just a few weeks after she'd found her father. That's what I said to my daughter that same afternoon, that maybe Sofia was trying to swear that that man, my husband, was hers, so as to get what she really wanted."

"And what was that, can you tell me?"

"To bury her father, sir. And she did, she managed to do just that, just as I said to my daughters and daughters-in-law, that's what happened. Less than two days went by before she'd accomplished what she'd set out to. Now the old man is resting in his own grave. It was then that I understood that I couldn't wait any longer, that I had to obey God's command, and I drew up that petition."

"And it never occurred to you to do it sooner?"

"I'm not a man, sir, I have no way of knowing what one does in situations like this."

"And what do you think, my good madam, of the fact that along with you thirty-six other women have presented similar petitions concerning their sons, husbands, uncles, fathers, brothers, and brothers-in-law?"

"I don't think anything, sir."

"Doesn't it seem to you a bit suspicious?"

"Why should it seem suspicious, sir?"

The captain slammed his fist on the desk. "Don't answer questions with questions, you old fox. We know your tricks. Answer when you're asked. How long do you think we can put up with this lack of respect for authority."

"Captain, I am a woman. I would expect that an officer of the nation's army wouldn't use violent methods and foul language against a woman. I'm merely exercising my rights. When I married, I swore to be faithful to my husband until death do us part. They've murdered my husband, who was mayor of this village, and I don't want anything more for the moment than to give him a funeral worthy of the life he offered me and my children and of the heights of service he rendered to the community."

"Your husband was a scoundrel," said the lieutenant, suddenly angry. "Did you know that? He was a criminal, an unscrupulous man, a traitor to his country."

"My husband isn't present, sir, to answer that accusation. If he were here, alive, he would answer like a man. I know he wouldn't want me to answer for him, he always asked me to remain calm and conduct myself like the woman I am, his woman, a man who knew how to read and write, respected by all, including his adversaries. I'm proud to have shared my life with Andrei Theogonafis."

"Enough speeches, enough speeches," ordered the captain. "Answer the question, ma'am. Don't you think it's strange that thirty-seven families should coincidentally present in three days' time petitions soliciting the burial of the same dead man who, a week before, had been claimed by only one, a woman who hadn't even seen the body? I suppose this seems absolutely normal to you?"

"The times we're living in aren't normal, sir. Or do you find it normal that I have no man in my house, that two of my sons have been shot, that my daughters have no one to marry, that my husband comes floating down the river after having been arrested in the capital some two years ago when he made an attempt to track down Theodoro Sarakis?"

"And the other women? What should I tell the other women?"

"That's your business, sir. I didn't study to be a judge in order to know what you should tell them."

"Mrs. Theogonafis, you realize that if I grant the request of one of you, the rest are going to be left without a relative to bury. Do you realize the injustice I'd be committing?"

"Sir, I'm glad you are so concerned with justice. That gives us a lot of hope. Because you yourself have the file on my husband, his disappearance, and now you can close the case."

"I advise you, madam," said the judge, going pale, "that my judgment was confirmed by the Court of Appeals. Your husband was not taken prisoner in my jurisdiction. That I can assure you."

"Another question," said the captain impatiently. "Before you conceived and then delivered this request, didn't Sofia Angelos come to see you?"

"Sofia Angelos did not come to see me, no, sir."

"Some member of her family, then?"

"Yes, sir. Her daughter-in-law Yanina came to see me."

"And what did you talk about?"

"About the dead man, sir."

"Yanina came to suggest that you should present this petition. Admit it, we have proof. Admit that Yanina came to make that suggestion, that all this is nothing more than a contrivance."

She blinked her eyes rapidly and rose in her seat. "Yanina was worried, sir, because she thought her mother-in-law had made a mistake, that that man could not be Michael Angelos and that that mistake could be serious for all of us, sir. She's sick over the fate of her husband Serguei, that's what was the matter with her. She never suggested anything to me. It was only after I confided that I, in my heart of hearts, was sure that the man we had found in the river was my own husband, Andrei, it wasn't till then that she said the only way to clear up this matter was by way of the judiciary, sir."

"And why didn't you come to see the captain?" asked the lieutenant.

"Because the captain had already declared that the body belonged to no one. It was impossible to change his opinion. With your permission, Lieutenant, but you know military men are like that. Look at Captain Gheorghakis, under whom you yourself served, sir."

"And it doesn't seem strange to you," the lieutenant continued, "that this same Yanina has spoken with seven other claimants, and that one Alexandra has spoken with eight more, and that one Cristina, daughter of Sofia, with several others, and one Hilda, and one Rosa, and so on and so forth, the thing never stops. Does it really seem to you the most natural thing that they've set out to convince all the neighboring families of the necessity of this action? Do you think they would be able to have done something like this without the consent, more like the active collaboration, of this troublemaking woman?"

"I'm going to tell you, sir, that it doesn't seem to me we're here to discuss Sofia Angelos's activities. I haven't the slightest idea of what is happening at her house. She's a good woman, a bit stubborn and willful, but those are virtues in times like these, a good woman who's been courteous to me all my life. What interests us is to straighten out the problem of my husband, sir."

"So you're truly convinced that that man was your husband? Before God, you're convinced?"

"If it's not true, Captain, sir, give him back to me alive, or tell me what prison he's in so I can go visit him and take him some food and clothes. Or give me his body so we can honor him as a husband and father and citizen. But don't ask me to fail again in my sacred duty and not bury him when he's right in front of my eyes, when he's in my hands."

"And if your husband appeared in that doorway," demanded the captain, his tone intensifying, "if I clapped my hands like this"—and he clapped loudly—"and he appeared right now in that doorway, what would you say to me?"

For the first time during the exchange, she hesitated, and something broke in her voice, in her bearing.

"I'd say thank you, Captain, if you give him back to me alive."

The door swung open and the orderly stepped in.

"Captain?"

"Your Honor, what do you say?"

"Next," said the judge. "I hope lunch is worth all this."

chapter four

⸙ vi ⸙

By the time dessert came, they were already on familiar terms.

"So you're not going to let me in on the big surprise?" she said to him.

The captain grazed her hand as if in passing, but didn't manage to get hold of it. "You're doubly curious, aren't you? Professionally and as a woman."

"My curiosity," she said indignantly, but softening that indignation by playing with her dessert spoon with that marvelous hand that had just escaped his, "is one hundred percent professional. All reporters have to be born like this—men, women, and queers—impossible, bothersome, nosy as a bloodhound snooping out the facts."

"And your feminine curiosity?" The captain elegantly poured her another glass of the rosé that he'd had brought on the double from the regiment's wine cellar.

"That," she answered, almost inaudibly, "I reserve for its full exercise...outside of working hours."

"How splendid! Someone who's able to keep the public and private realms distinct."

"Only up to a point. All of a sudden the damned zones intersect and one can't tell which to believe. But there's an infallible method for finding out where you are. Know what it is?"

"I haven't the slightest."

"In my private life, *my* Captain, it's I who provide the surprises, and then..."

"And then...?"

"And then I realize that I'm no longer acting as a reporter."

"And that must make someone else curious."

"Let's put it that way. Some other person."

At first the captain thought it strange that a woman would be sent to a province that less than six months ago had still been regarded as a combat zone, where the dangers were such that all requests by journalists to attend the theater of operations were uniformly rejected, but it was clear that the army's public relations office knew what it was doing. Everything had been thought out down to the last detail.

The first brief news items concerning the unusual petition that had come to be known as "the case of the thirty-seven widows" had gotten past the vigilant eyes of the censors by assuming a jocular tone, harmlessly appearing in a gossip column of one of the dailies in the capital. As it turned out, it provided a field day for the commentators. In a little mountain village whose name mattered to no one and which wasn't even on the map, a sizable group of women was fighting over nothing less than a corpse. In the absence of men, cadavers will do, was the ironic interpretation of one writer. An unprecedented case of collective bigamy, of unusual proportions, added another: the dead man was plenty macho about his business. In any case, summed up a columnist on some lost page of an insignificant daily, it was something unheard of before in this country or any other. We finally broke the record for something, since we always do so badly in sports competitions, more widows per corpse than anyplace else. Although it hadn't yet turned into anything more than this, and the news was fading as the days went by, the public relations people—with their legendary sense of smell—had got wind of other interested parties who might be weaving their webs. Who could tell when the matter would spill over in new directions, religious, legal, even political, opening other matters by way of interpretation, treading forbidden ground, distilling the poison which the press, insolent and even encouraged by the recent liberal measures of the government in its phase of national reconciliation, had stored up over the years. Therefore, without either completely suppressing the news, advising the respective commentators to be more careful about what they wrote, or stressing too much what was worrying them, it was decided to send some trusted correspondent from the Sunday staff of *The News*, the largest and oldest paper in the country, to enlighten public opinion, especially that of women, concerning the truth of the matter.

"We hope you're going to make the army look good," that voice from public relations said to the captain, with an undefinable relish that bothered him. "Be sure to put in a good performance."

"I'll do what I can," he answered, wondering about the meaning of that suggestive tone, but no one was listening anymore at the other end of the line.

Two days later, when her legs and then her hips slipped out of the car that brought her, he suddenly understood. And she, for her part, was more than frank. Almost immediately, and point-blank, she'd asked the captain if he was surprised at her appearance, and if he wouldn't have preferred a man. Such aggressiveness and audacity in a handsome woman ended up softening the captain's defenses as well as his voice, and he didn't try to answer right away. He feasted his eyes on the simple miracle of her existence in a place like this.

"The army, miss," he'd finally responded, "has secured this district. We have established optimum conditions to guarantee the safety of you or any other journalist, of whatever sex. But it's easy for whoever visits us, especially in the case, as here, of persons who have not had nor been able to have, nor it is hoped will have the experience of war and its vicissitudes, to overlook the fact that only a short while ago crimes and incursions were occurring daily in this very spot, and that the husbands of these same women that you are going to interview and who are now crying and raising petitions and exhibiting probatory photographs, those husbands themselves are the ones responsible for the criminal and terrorist activities against the country which have obliged the armed forces to intervene with the efficiency and virility for which we are known and feared."

"What a speech, Captain! So you would have preferred a man." He smiled gallantly. "The truth is, yes, I would have preferred one. I would have. Now, however, I must advise you that my outlook has changed."

"So soon? And how do you account for this change?"

As if the bitch didn't know how he accounted for it, as if females didn't learn the science of flirtation before birth, as if the way she... But the captain preferred to cut off the course of his elaborations. He'd take full control of this affair. It was necessary to keep his ideas on ice, to imagine nothing, absolutely nothing. Because this hunk of woman was the kind that winds up reading a man's mind. He regained the appropriately professional tone. He believed, he said in substance, that an educated woman was in an exceptionally good position to appreciate the underlying causes of this situation. It wasn't only a matter of there being a conspiracy—there was, that was clearly evident—but of comprehending the backward mental and emotional state the inhabitants of places like this were stuck in, with their pagan customs, their age-old ignorance, their marginal existence almost untouched by the benefits of contemporary civilization. This barbarism constituted the only valid explanation for these poor women allowing themselves to be manipulated by the enemy, contriving to dirty the cleanest thing they had, their sacred links to home, family, the veneration of their ancestors, honor, in an absurd and senseless adventure.

She calmly took it all down in her notebook. Still writing, she asked, "Do you have a family, Captain? You defend it so zealously."

Without hesitating, he opened his desk and passed her the photo of his wife and three children.

"How pretty they are," she said, returning the photo.

He put it away before proceeding. "Besides, I suppose you know that you've arrived at a very opportune moment, most propitious, I'd say. I don't know if they explained to you in public relations that, on the occasion of your visit, we're going to demonstrate publicly the falseness of the assertions of these women."

"They told me so, Captain, but they didn't offer details. I don't know what it's about."

"It's about the fact, which you will be able to verify, and later publicize, that this is nothing more than a maneuver, a well-mounted deception."

"Could you be a bit more explicit?"

"Since you haven't been informed of the matter, the truth is I prefer that it be a surprise. Let's just say that it's a little surprise that no one's expecting, not those women nor you either."

"A surprise?"

"We could call it a present for you, if you don't take it the wrong way," the captain said to her. "It's always good to offer a reward to those who make an effort not only to understand the difficulties of the current situation, but also to transmit that understanding to their readers."

"Thanks for the pretty words, but if you can tell me what the famous surprise consists of, then I'd really be grateful."

"If I were to announce it"—the captain rose from his seat—"it would end up ruining the pleasure, the joy and delight, of perceiving the news in all its fresh originality. If you can wait until after lunch..."

"Lunch will not sit well with me, Captain. I won't be able to do a proper interview."

"We have time."

"I have to leave this afternoon. We don't have as much time as you say."

"We'll see about that," said the captain.

vii

"I've got them all together, Captain," said the sergeant, "as you ordered."

"And they've also been informed there'll be a reporter present," added the lieutenant, shooting her a glance without much enthusiasm.

"And the rest?"

"All ready, sir."

"Then let's go in."

The school was one large room, the only one, other than the church, that could hold that many people. The villagers had built it themselves, Father Gabriel had explained, working Sundays and even nights. When everything was ready, the government had given a hand with the painting and some high functionary from the Ministry of Education had come to inaugurate the building. Since then, the hall had been used for festivals, fairs, dances, and municipal and political meetings. Now it was full of women, the thirty-seven petitioners seated or standing, in a motionless silence. They looked at the military men with the same mixture of hatred and indifference as always, extremely detached, yet intimate. The presence of a woman among the soldiers didn't seem to have an effect on them, insofar as she'd come from the other side of the mountains and was wearing clothes whose tone, color, and cut they'd rarely seen, nothing like their own mourning.

"Quiet," shouted the lieutenant, although no one was talking.

The captain got up from his schoolteacher's seat behind the table. From here the high functionary from the Ministry of Education had made his speech, but that was to another public. Husbands were present, children, nervous adolescents, families.

"Very well. We are pleased and happy to have with us today the presence of a lady reporter from *The News*. I don't expect that you have ever read this newspaper, although its prestige extends even to a place like this, but perhaps you're aware that it is the most important one in our country and enjoys considerable international prestige as well. She has made this difficult and exhausting journey because there is interest in your case. The public, like the judge, has found the matter we're all familiar with as incredible as we have. Later, the young lady will have the opportunity to ask you questions which you'll be able to answer freely. As a result, I'm going to request that you remain here after my talk, so that you'll be able to converse with the press."

The photographer, who was at the back of the room, next to the sergeant, snapped a picture. The flash lit up the women, who turned around, frightened.

The captain smiled. "But I've brought you together for another purpose. I've insisted, at each of our meetings, since the first time I spoke with one of you two days after I took command here, I have insisted that this mania for burying men who have nothing to do with your families is truly some kind of madness. I would even dare to qualify it as a collective hysteria." He noticed that the reporter was taking down every word. "Collective hysteria," he repeated with emphatic satisfaction. A woman decides to identify a corpse that's been completely destroyed by the river current. She wants so badly to find her loved one that she ventures to recognize him under confused circumstances. The nation's army understands that feeling and agrees, in a moment of generosity that does us honor, to grant a funeral to the anonymous victim. The army understands that when a family lives in uncertainty and instability, it is common that they should desire to do away with these feelings however they can, in order thus to resume the normal course of everyday life. They would rather see the father dead and buried than imagine him suffering the rigors of some presumed punishment, or lost out there in the mountains, or even finished off by his own fanatical colleagues in some desolate spot from which he will never return. We military men know what it is to live like this, because our own women and our own children, our mothers and fathers, have had to become accustomed with heroic self-denial to these kinds of emotions. But that's how war is, ladies, and you're all well aware that it wasn't our armed forces who started this dispute. This region was prosperous and peaceful until some of its inhabitants, stirred up by sinister passions and foreign ideas, decided to desecrate this country's legitimate authority and to sabotage the mission of national unity which the forces of order had imposed when we were faced with our land's moral, and even physical, decay."

The captain stepped down from the platform and walked out into the assembly. His boots stopped now and then beside one of the women, nearly touching her. Finally he stationed himself next to the old woman poised at the edge of a seat almost at the very center of the hall.

"But I told you that what you were claiming was absurd. I asked you what would that man say, that same man you insisted on burying, if he returned home to find himself dead, not at our hands, although we would have been justified in killing him, but at the hands of his own loved ones, who had given him a funeral, a cross, a religious service. And then here he is alive and healthy. I asked you what would be the indignant reaction of that man, what suspicions he would end up harboring. I told you that it was my opinion, and that of our nation's army too, that we were dealing here with a conspiracy, that you were being used by enemies of the country to sow discontent, demand the impossible, stir up nonsense. Didn't I say that to you? Didn't I speak to you as a friend, with true sympathy, as there ought to be among fellow citizens, each and every one of us devoted to the common cause of patriotic reconstruction?"

The women were silent.

"All right, my esteemed ladies, the time has come to show you my words were true. Some of you have thought and even said that what this captain wants is for us to give up worrying about this matter so he can gain a little time. That's what you've said and thought. I'm going to prove to you it wasn't so. The Supreme Government has become interested in every one of you, in every single mother of this generous land we have the honor of living in together. And that's because, for the nation's army, there is nothing more sacred than woman and nothing greater than motherhood. It is in defense of that woman and of the values of the home which she seeks to preserve above all else that we have always acted. That woman is the sweetheart, the wife, the mother of the fatherland. You are about to see that I wasn't lying to you and that we've always kept your problems resolutely in our hearts. The Supreme Government, like a benevolent father, knows how to punish and how to forgive. The reconciliation and family peace that we've proclaimed is not merely so many words on paper. And you'll have proof of that in just a few minutes."

The captain returned to the platform, walking backward, in such a way that his eyes, sliding from one impassive face to another, did not for an instant give up command of the scene, as if defying them to say something. As he took them all in panoramically, something like a grin began to sketch itself on his mouth. He half leaned, half sat on the edge of the table, then bent toward the reporter who was writing, twisting his neck in such a way that his watchful head still took in the room, and he said, lowering his voice, "Promises are promises. Now, Irene, comes the surprise." He snapped to attention, with the decisive voice of command: "Sergeant!"

"Captain!"

"Proceed, Sergeant."

Not one of the women made half a turn to observe how the sergeant, in back, opened one of the double doors and went out. It was as if the captain hadn't even given that order. From outside, they heard the shout of the sergeant and like a strange echo, the prompt and distant sound of a truck or perhaps a car starting down the hill.

Without taking his eyes off them, the captain again leaned slowly toward the reporter, till his lips stopped barely above her hair, careful not to touch it.

"Don't say I didn't warn you. You won't be able to leave today."

"May I ask why not?"

"Because now you'll have to interview someone. Someone more or less special, under the circumstances."

"A man?"

"Always so curious."

"A man?"

"He's of the male sex, but whether or not he's a man..."

"And that's the big surprise?"

"That's the little surprise. Don't expect more."

An army truck pulled up in front of the windows. The women turned their heads in unison toward the outside, gradually, as if they weren't overly interested, as if they could tell from experience they'd be able to see no more than the vague silhouette of the driver against the malignant light. A fine cloud of dust filtered into the hall and blurred what was happening. Then the truck disappeared, turning the corner. The screeching of brakes could be heard. The measured ballet of the women's faces turned toward the captain.

"And them?" the reporter asked, still whispering, almost in the captain's ear, so that he could feel the touch of her breath.

"What about them?"

"I came to speak with them. When will I be able to?"

"Later, much later. First the other interview, the surprise."

She raised her voice slightly, impatient, but no one else could hear her. "I can't. I have business in the city first thing in the morning."

The captain controlled his words, kept them quiet, calm, domesticated, almost inaudible. "Sometimes," he said, eyeing the stubborn figure of Sofia seated there in the hall, "one can't carry out all one's plans. Other times, yes. Other times things turn out like one never even dreamed they would. But don't worry, Irene, we'll put you up like a princess."

Just then the door opened and the sergeant came in.

"Ready, sir. At your command."

Before the captain could answer, the reporter spoke. He could sense the cool but mounting fury caught in her throat. He could hear her agitated breathing.

"I must go today, Captain. And no one can change my mind. I hope you understand that."

The captain began to sweep his gaze across the faces of the women, pausing easily to rest on every one, ending again on the old Angelos woman, lingering on her worn black dress. She kept her eyes fixed on some empty, nonexistent spot on the wall.

"That's how things are, Madam Sofia," the captain suddenly boomed out. "One can't always carry out all one's plans. That's life."

The old woman didn't acknowledge the reference.

The captain reached out his hand and picked up the pencil the reporter had set temporarily on the table. The captain used it to signal to the sergeant.

"Captain!"

"Bring in the prisoner."

For about two seconds there was absolute stillness, as if everyone were waiting for all the traces of the captain's words to disappear. Then the women jumped to their feet and turned toward the door. They began rustling, buzzing.

"Quiet!" shouted the lieutenant. "Nobody in here moves without permission."

The captain kept his eyes on the old one. She was the only one who hadn't moved. Very carefully and with great dignity, now she rose and turned her back on him to look, with the rest of the women, at the door of the hall through which the man called "the prisoner" would enter.

The photographer extravagantly shot off his flash.

Then the captain shoved back his chair and fixed his eyes on the reporter.

"No," the captain said, handing her pencil back and smiling slightly. "Tomorrow. You'll leave tomorrow."

chapter five

viii

Grandma didn't want anyone else to go and wait for Serguei, nobody else, not even his twin sister Cristina. Only Yanina and the baby, and he should be prettied up to meet his papa, these things happen only once in a lifetime. We didn't protest. It was right that the two of them, the three of them, should be alone before meeting with the whole family.

Grandma had gone directly up to Yanina when she returned, not responding to our greetings or questions. "Take off those widow's clothes, child, and dress up the baby nicely."

Yanina was next to me. I could feel the trembling passing through my own body, a shaking that started in her hips and rose to her eyes. They seemed to shine, a light flaring up in her, and we saw her get up, we saw her go over to Grandma and take her hand.

"Serguei? Is it Serguei, Mama?"

Grandma smiled and said yes, yes indeed, girl. Her husband was fully alive, in good health. She'd wanted to bring him to her right away, as soon as he'd come in through the door of the school, but the captain had said he was still the one giving the orders and first the reporter had to do an interview with him and only then would he be set free. Conditionally free, the lieutenant had added, looking at each woman and at her especially.

"Cristina," Yanina said, "it's Serguei, Serguei's coming, you told me so, you told me he was alive, you told me so, bless you."

And the captain had also advised Grandma that it was likely the same reporter would want to ask her a few questions, so would she and the rest please be kind enough to remain where they were until the prisoner returned. But she had answered that her family did not discuss their problems in public and did not give interviews, much less to strangers, and as far as she was concerned she was going, in order to let her daughter-in-law and grandchild know, in the light of the fact that the army hadn't had the decency to tell them that her son was on the way and preferred to put on a big spectacle instead of granting them a relieved and peaceful night. Then Grandma had approached Serguei. We imagined her drawing closer to him step by step to hug him or kiss him or caress him or simply touch him to prove he was real, and the captain had barked an order, and they took him away. So Yanina should hurry. They were letting him go any minute, the interview was taking place in the captain's office.

Yanina went right into the house and we heard her speaking in a shaky voice to the sleeping baby, waking him up gently. I followed her to the door and saw her beside his crib, singing to him with that beautiful voice of hers, something like wake up my little walnut, my little almond, wake up my ripe little fruit, your daddy lives, your daddy's coming, listen to the poplars, your papa's coming, Papa's alive. Then she lifted him in her arms and, seeing me, passed him to me to be washed and dressed.

Mama and Grandma stayed outside. I listened to them while I cleaned up the baby, who had begun to cry with his eyes wide open and surprised and still sleepy.

"So you didn't speak to him, Grandma?" Mama asked. "Neither of you could say a thing."

And I didn't want to think about it. We didn't want to pay any attention because water had to be fetched for Yanina and we had to help her dig out her green dress, the one she'd never worn, with the flamboyant orange trim, the one that Serguei had given her when he found out she was expecting a baby after so many years of wanting one without any luck, telling her it was for after the baby's arrival, that he bought it now so she would remember the shape her body would be after the birth, so neither of them would forget that as she got bigger. A few months later they'd come to take Serguei and Dimitriou away, and no, Fidelia didn't want to think about what her mama was really asking. Because what she was asking and what I was asking and my brother when he got there and didn't want to let filter into our heads now since we had to relish that little bit of pine-scented soap reserved for special occasions and Yanina who looked at the green dress somewhere between bewitchment and disbelief, as if it simply wasn't real and the black cloth she was wearing had already turned to a swirl of ashes. What had to be asked was something else, which Grandma had left out, but it was impossible. We imagined the captain and the lieutenant and the sergeant and that idiot photographer blinding them with his flashbulbs and on top of that the orderly who'd go tell Sarakis and that whore Cecilia everything and that strange woman up on the platform who maybe was even the captain's wife, and Grandma hadn't been able to ask and Alexandra didn't ask her either. They couldn't say anything, she had said that much. She hadn't asked if he was all right since he seemed all there and healthy enough, although too skinny and awfully pale. He looked at the floor without returning her glance as if he were still a prisoner, and hadn't even asked the other kinds of questions that one thinks of in those situations, like how had the trip been or had he missed the family, things that Yanina would surely be asking as they walked back from town. So you didn't speak to him, Grandma, Alexandra had said with that sense of, I would have asked him, would have asked him even though all the women in town were present, all the women in the universe. What shame could there be in asking what we all had on the tip of our tongue? We don't air family matters in public. She didn't want to give the captain satisfaction, although in reality the victory was ours. What sense was there in thinking we'd been defeated, that the captain had managed to bend us? It was they who'd been forced to do it, let go of at least one of our men and now perhaps they were also going to have to...but that was precisely the question that Grandma hadn't asked. Perhaps Yanina would pose it to him before we did, perhaps she was wondering about it right now while I without knowing what to do with my knees and heels and these pigeons of joy and dread trapped in our chests, that question that at some point along the road even Yanina would have to bring up in our name, after talking about the dress and showing him each funny trick of little Serguei, the same question she'd have put to any other man in the family who'd come back alone, hands tied, head bowed, paler and more elusive than the moon, that question, the same one, the one that Grandma hadn't asked, that Alexandra couldn't ask, that all of us turned back on our tongues like a chewed pit whose juice was gone and we didn't know where to spit it, that question, that one.

Then Yanina, with a clumsy decisive gesture, undid the black, letting it fall at her feet like a wrinkled, dead, smelly dog, and her body appeared in the shadows, and from where I was I could see Mama's eyes as she watched Yanina naked, Mama and Grandma and I all seeing her out of mourning, revealing her white, sinewy body, all these months under the same cloth every one of us wore except Fidelia, her breasts standing out, and we didn't know which of us remembered the herbs, it must have been Rosa, who'd never had a sweetheart, it must have been Rosa who remembered the herbs that Yanina had gathered in the evenings, the herbs she'd crushed to create the incomparable scents her mother had taught her, when you're grown, Fidelia, when you've grown all that you must, when you're ready to marry, when you love a sturdy man, I'm going to give you this and even hand over the secret of how to mix it, and she let me smell it and its perfume carried me off beyond the fields, the cherry blossoms, every evening she went out looking, went with Cristina to reaffirm her faith that Serguei would come back, and Cristina who was thinking about Serguei and also about her own boyfriend Aristos, and who was now perhaps also remembering Aristos as she brought the water for Yanina, and she had to have felt the weight of our eyes like a kind of soap or water running over her body shining in that half-light, must have felt the sleek skin of her body too exposed, stood there an instant without looking back, permitting our eyes on her skin, on the dead pile of clothes at her feet, her feet sticking out like two hot flowers. It must have been like waking up to another reality, falling into the question Grandma hadn't, off that cliff, and she said to Cristina that she didn't need any more water and would Maria hand her the cloth to dry herself, and she turned around and I noticed that Grandma had already gone outside, and Mama and I kept looking at that powerful back, the haunches rippling under that gorgeous waist, as she quickly put on the dress and went to the mirror. Then she came over to Fidelia and in a deep, clear voice thanked her for taking care of the baby, and took him from me. I'd almost forgotten I was holding him, I scarcely knew how my hands had automatically soothed him and cleaned him and dressed him, how he had just hung there all that time while his mother was getting ready.

"You can brush your hair on the way," Cristina said, pushing her, if she didn't hurry she'd be late. Yanina took the brush as if she couldn't remember what it was, as if she didn't spend an hour every night brushing her hair, now a black cascade falling softly and intensely, accented by the green with the orange trim. Sometimes she let Fidelia brush it while she spoke to her of when she'd be grown and have a sweetheart, that I had to promise her I'd never let him go away, not to war nor to look for work in the city, that you had to take care of a young man like your very own body. But now we no longer went over the candidates. For years the sweetheart had been somebody far away, nonexistent. Perhaps he'd come from the other side of the hill, I'd have to care for him like my own body. "On the way," Cristina repeated.

Yanina looked herself over in the mirror one last time and walked out to the patio. We followed. She stopped there for a minute, perhaps expecting us to give her a message or additional advice, that we'd send Serguei something through her or maybe she just wanted to talk something over with us, explain something.

Nobody tried or knew what to say.

"I hope it goes well," Alexandra whispered at last, because Mama couldn't leave her like that, so quiet and alone. I hope it goes well.

She waited long enough to get the baby settled and nobody said anything else and another second and then she turned with a shake of her shining hair.

"Just a minute," said Grandma. Yanina stopped. "Just a minute," Grandma repeated and went running into the house, coming back out at once with a bag. She showed her what was in it. Bread, some cold cuts, goat cheese, grapes, tomatoes.

Yanina nodded her head. Of course, he'd be hungry. And then we watched her walk off, relieved, grateful, with the bag under her arm and the brush in the same hand and the little one looking back at us over his mother's shoulder.

Then Grandma sat down and after that we all sat down and didn't look at each other except for a sidelong glance. Nobody wanted to add another word, like in one of those games where whoever speaks first loses, all of us stricken with the same plague of silence. Until then it had been Yanina we were busy with. We'd let her invade and saturate our thoughts and feelings, bustling about after hairbrushes and clothes and water and bread and tripping over each other even when there wasn't that much to do, since there wasn't room for anything more than she getting herself ready to go to Serguei alive. Even Grandma hadn't wanted to fracture that little happiness Yanina had a right to, come what might, even if so many unanswered questions hung there dying in the air like shadows in search of their bodies. It was the way when a tragedy happens the first thing one thinks of is how to keep the children from finding out, how to explain it to the children.

But Yanina was gone and we were left, pieces of a wheel which had suddenly lost their axle or the pretext to make them turn and move ahead, still terribly anxious to go on wherever, all of us here with nobody else to talk to, while darkness slowly fell, not able to stop thinking about that question, and the farther away Yanina got, the more room there was for what we'd been thinking, like when the children are finally in bed and you can let go and cry, be a grown-up and let out your pain. So we stayed there, stunned by our own immobility and nobody would even look up when one of us suddenly made a move to get up or say something. We knew we wouldn't move, we wouldn't speak until Yanina came back.

And she took a long time, she'd be hours and hours, not only because she'd be anxious to be alone with Serguei as long as possible or because we imagined Serguei taking a long and circuitous route, but because the other women would be guarding the exit, crowded around the captain's office, not to answer the stupid questions of some reporter who didn't have any man missing in her family, but to ask questions themselves, to ask Serguei precisely the ones neither Grandma nor Alexandra nor I nor any of us, questions to which they had the right as much as Yanina had the right to a few hours of peace, the same right the baby had to know his father. They wouldn't keep silent and proud like Grandma, because Serguei wasn't just the only man in our family to return in a year, but the only man in the town and the whole region and for who knows how many miles around, so pretty soon, maybe tomorrow, other women would begin arriving, ones who hadn't been at the school, they'd begin arriving at our house, a few at a time at first, and more in a few days from farther away, from small farms and villages and hills and ravines, they'd come for who knows how many months, to ask the questions Grandma hadn't asked at the school, sisters and wives would come and grandmothers too, aunts and cousins and sweethearts and widows and even lovers. We didn't like to imagine the faces they would come with, their bruised looks, it was like our own image wandering over the roads, if news had come to us that in some worthless little settlement a hundred or two hundred or five hundred miles away a prisoner had appeared, any of us would have set out on foot, by mule, however, selling everything we had to find out something, they'd start arriving tomorrow.

So we just let it get dark. Not one of us wanted to get up and fix something to eat, devoured by the fear that we'd say something else, do something else with our hands and our legs and our teeth. The sky was turning a clear violet. Not even the perfect, pink, innocent clouds up there, nor later the stars so fiercely clean could ease our solitude.

When each of us could scarcely see the others, we began to relax, loosen our neck muscles. Without other eyes on our faces, we all perceived the change in Grandma, understood it better than if we'd been watching in broad daylight. Like milk going sour, the joy that bathed us for a minute was dimming out. A burnt black liquid was rising to the surface, all the more persistent for having been hidden or ignored. Any minute, soon, as Serguei's and Yanina's steps approached by whatever detours they'd taken, soon, Grandma would have to do it, wouldn't have the excuse of the captain or the reporter or the orderly or whoever, nor could she give Yanina all the time Yanina would have given Alexandra if Dimitriou had been the one, Grandma getting harder and more severe and bitter in her seat there next to us. A part of her was dying as if she were a stone slowly crumbling under the ground, more than worried by the inevitable question, more than exhausted by not knowing how she would ask it, how and where it would break from her throat, more than that, what Grandma didn't know, perhaps didn't want to know, was what her reaction would be once Serguei answered, Grandma, who could sense my look of a wounded swallow and the distant, now suffocating desperation of Alexandra.

That's how we remained, these feelings passing around among ourselves like some contagious bottle in which you spit instead of drink, everything that would happen as soon as Serguei arrived, with no time to rest, however much we'd dreamed of nothing but his return, the return of one of our men, finally a man in the house and not just Alexis trying to be. It had to happen before tomorrow morning, before the other women would start arriving. If Alexandra, if Fidelia, if any of us would have walked hundreds of miles to ask a total stranger, someone just like Serguei, how could we not do it with him in our own house, hugging him, crying with grief and relief, his sisters and aunt and sister-in-law and wife and niece, walking with Yanina in the direction of the question boiling on Grandma's lips, about to arrive.

There we were, dead still, for hours and hours it must have been. We were holding vigil over a, but nobody wanted to think it. Was it possible that we weren't expecting the return of someone alive, but Yanina bringing home a corpse she'd dragged from town, knowing as time stretched out that we would never have to hear Serguei's answer? Why would they have let him go and not the others, why him and not the rest, and where had he been, the certainty of his evasion, his silence growing so big no question could be asked. I tried to stop the thought that condemned him from filtering through before he could even defend himself, tried to summon the image of my uncle, tried to rescue moments when he'd taken me and Alexis fishing in the river, the river where now, and always I came back to the same thing, Grandpa facedown on the sand, that hawk-faced lieutenant asking my name and looking at my legs, with Grandpa's face like the moon hidden and torn by some weak yellow clouds. I tried to count the stars, wanting again to be the girl discovering faces and night-time mysteries in the arms of her uncle Serguei, but the only face I could trace was my father's out there somewhere, the only mystery his absence. Then I looked at my hands and conjured up a doll, the one Serguei had made me. It took him hours with those quiet craftsman's hands to make it for Fidelia, and Yanina had sewn it a rough little dress, and I couldn't avoid remembering that I had run to show it to Papa. Dimitriou picked it up, admired his brother's skill, praised his talent. He was wasting his time as a farmer; with those hands he could earn a living in the city, every memory ending up mixed with Dimitriou or the other men, as if Serguei were the only one of them dead, the only one who could never come back. We felt all the women who'd been at the school were watching with us in the darkness, we had the sensation that the one coming down the road was Papa, Grandpa, Aristos, any other man than Serguei.

All of a sudden, like a slap that shakes you out of a daydream, without our having heard footsteps, there stood Serguei under the moonlight, waves and waves of moonlight, Serguei more alive than any memory of Dimitriou or the others, with his son asleep in his arms. For an instant the ghostly light shook our eyes and we couldn't recognize him, couldn't see how he handed the little one to Yanina, how he wavered slightly before the women. We'd all stood up. For an instant, Serguei didn't know who to go up to. We were all identical, a single tormented, extended body. Then he opened his arms and silently went toward Grandma, but she didn't move toward him. She even took a step back and Serguei stopped halfway across the shadows to be sure it was she who'd done that, and for the first time in hours someone said something, Grandma had to speak.

"Did you sign anything?" that's what she asked him, that, and several of us remembered the words of Grandma's father, who had announced one night that the only thing he would never do was sign a piece of paper they'd put in front of him. Years ago he'd been through this. They'd taken him in and held him for months, and here we saw him, Karoulos Mylonas, able to survive, living proof, and afterwards, from a distance, it was much less terrible then what one might have imagined before it happened, and if at any time a document was brought to any of them, to any of us, his family, a document which had his signature where he'd confessed something, even something he'd really done, we were not to believe it, because his signature was like his shadow, he'd never give it to any man. They, the men, his son-in-law Michael and his three grandsons—Dimitriou, Serguei, and Themi—had understood, and we, the women who were standing back a little ways listening, took note of that although it was for the men. We said to ourselves that no one in this family, man or woman, not even children like Fidelia and Alexis, would give up a breath, it was understood. Not the scratch of a pencil, nothing.

Although Grandma had skipped the question that every one of the thirty-six women waiting outside the office, everyone of us, had wanted to ask and the one that would begin tomorrow morning, and the one that Alexandra now, we waited for Serguei's answer.

Yanina stepped forward, her hair shining almost white in that impossible light. "Mama, he had nothing to do with all this politics. He never got involved in these things, you know that, Papa knew it and Dimitriou too and you yourself."

Grandma took another step back.

"What did you sign?" she asked.

"Mama, they took him away because he was from this family. The only thing he wanted was to live quietly."

Grandma looked at her tenderly, half smiling, a grimace of a smile. A look that said everything. It was good that a woman should always stand by her man, that was very good. She was pleased Serguei had found a girl so loyal, the right mother for his son. But Yanina had not grown up in this house, Yanina couldn't understand. It wasn't her fault, just a fact. There were things she couldn't understand.

But Yanina wasn't going to keep still. She went up to Serguei with the baby in her arms, got as close to him as she could, gloriously green in the shadows.

"What was he going to sign, Mama? What was he going to sign, if he couldn't tell them anything? He had nothing to tell them. He wasn't involved in anything. They hurt him, Mama, they hurt him and he wasn't involved in anything, he didn't know anything about anything, he didn't have a single secret to hand over. What document was he going to—"

Grandma interrupted with a gesture. She turned half around and went into the house. None of us followed. We didn't know what to do. Cristina went forward to embrace Serguei, but he looked at her strangely and she stopped there, close to him, frozen, watching.

"Tell her," Yanina begged us. "Tell her it's her son, he's back, he's back, and she—"

"If they killed him," said Alexandra suddenly. "Tell me Serguei, for the love of God, tell me. If you know something about Dimitriou..."

That question, that one.

Serguei went to the door and from there, before going in, he spoke for the first time. Another voice came out of him, not the one we'd anticipated, that we remembered from a year, two years ago.

"They keep you with a blindfold over your eyes," he said, "for five months. For five months they keep you like that. You don't see anyone, you speak to no one, nobody speaks to you. I could hardly remember Yanina's face."

And he went inside.

Grandma had opened the trunk where we keep the clothes. She was dusting off things to wear, the same as the other time, the time she informed us we had to go down to the river, the whole family had to get ready, had to hold vigil over Michael, hurry. This time she didn't say anything. She took out only her own clothes.

"Mama," said Serguei.

Grandma went on as if nothing, no one. She pulled out a dress, her best one, the one she wore to baptisms, weddings, big parties, moving her head maybe to remember something, calling someone back. Then she folded it again, smoothed it out, and put it back in the trunk.

"Yanina," Grandma called over the shoulder of her son who was almost beside her. "Yanina, Serguei is tired. I think it would be good if you let him sleep. Tomorrow's going to be a long day."

We all went in and saw her taking out the clothes and rearranging them.

"How can you be so hard, Sofia," said Hilda. "He's your son. He's the only one left alive."

"Dimitriou's going to come back," said Alexandra. "I know he's not dead. Serguei, isn't it true your brother's going to come back?"

"They split us up the next day," Serguei said, turning his back. "I haven't seen him since."

Serguei wasn't even speaking to her, simply repeating again and again the same story to any woman who asked him the same question. He was someplace else, not used to the idea that this was his own house, that he was facing his mother kneeling beside the trunk, his wife and child near him, his brother's wife asking the questions he'd been hearing all afternoon, that he'd have to answer again tomorrow and the next day and all the years to come.

"If something had happened to him, I'd know it," said Alexandra. "Yanina, I'd know it here inside. Yanina!"

Grandma had finished packing a little bundle of clothes she'd chosen. Now she got up and went to the table where the photos were. She took the one of her father, then of her husband, finally of Dimitriou, and placed them on top of the clothes at her feet. She looked at Serguei's photo. She turned her head to contemplate Serguei himself who was standing there, still without having moved, and put that photo with the others. As if that son were also a memory, someone who had to be kept in mind along with the rest of the men in the family.

Grandma went over to Yanina and took the bag out of her hands. She saw there was almost nothing left inside, some chunks of bread, a bit of cold meat. She looked for some cheese on the table, some more bread. "Fidelia, tomorrow you'll fetch me some eggs. Boil them and bring them to me, dear."

She took her packet and went toward the door. Before going out, she turned and pointed a finger in her sister's direction.

"Hilda's the one in charge. Until Alexis or I come back."

None of us wanted to look at Serguei.

"Where are you going, Mama?" asked Cristina, although we all knew the answer.

I didn't want to listen, the words that Fidelia and Alexandra had been afraid of since Grandma told Yanina to take off her mourning dress, we didn't want to be there to hear what Grandma had been preparing for all afternoon, from the instant Serguei came through the door of the school.

"Where am I going?" Grandma looked at Cristina surprised. "To the river, to the river, where else would I be going?"

"To the river?"

"Yes," she said, "to the river. I'm going to wait for my son."

chapter six

ix

"You can begin now," said the captain. "I'm very interested to know the details of your journey."

Everything had gone, said the orderly, just as the captain had wanted. The invitation was delivered. Philip Kastoria would come to the dinner. Only a little problem had arisen at the beginning.

"A little problem?"

Yes, sir. When they arrived, the orderly noticed that the guard at the main gate was a new person. He had commented on this to Cecilia. Of course, the guard didn't recognize him and had declared he had strict orders not to admit anyone. He would see to it that the letter was delivered.

"And what did you do?"

If the captain would permit him a comment, above all he had felt satisfied that the guards were properly fulfilling their duty of protecting the family and property of Philip Kastoria. But those orders had nothing to do with him, the new guard simply didn't know him. It was enough for the orderly to explain to the man who he was, since the guard had naturally heard of him, for everything to be straightened out. He'd opened the gate and accompanied him to the house. If the captain didn't mind him saying so, yes, he'd found that guard, and another with whom he'd had the chance to exchange a few words, a bit nervous. The groundless rumors had gotten even as far as them.

"Fine. And did you go to the house alone or did you take your girl friend along?"

No, sir. She'd stayed waiting in the jeep.

"And how long did your conversation with Mr. Kastoria last?"

Three hours.

When Emmanuel climbed back into the jeep, she didn't want to complain or ask him anything right away. He didn't say anything either, despite the fact that it was baking hot inside. The hours in the sun had scorched the driver's seat, and the steering wheel was practically untouchable. Still, he started the motor and turned the jeep around for the return trip. Before accelerating, he raised his hand in salute to the two guards watching them, rifles in hand, behind the main gate. Beyond them, the tall, blond, broad figure of Kastoria amiably waved good-bye. Emmanuel kicked at the accelerator and the vehicle leaped forward, roaring. A cool breeze blew in. Only when they'd passed the first curve, when the entry gate and the three men were out of sight, did he say to her, "You could have gotten out and sat in the shade, couldn't you?"

"You told me to stay here, so I did." She waited for him to respond, but since he added nothing, she asked, "What did you talk about?"

His voice sounded rough, like one of those infinitely dusty hills alongside the road. "Nothing. Men's business. Things that wouldn't interest you."

"Business of yours and I wouldn't be interested? How do you know?"

He didn't take his eyes off the road. Nothing in his voice changed when he said, "Because you're a woman, and women don't know anything about politics. That's why."

"Three hours," the captain repeated. "So Mr. Kastoria was there?"

Yes, sir. He had found him with his brother and his wife having tea in one of the salons. Would the captain like a detailed account of the conversation?

"Tell me everything."

Emmanuel took his eyes off the road for a second and shot her a sidelong glance. "I'd like to know just one thing. What's bothering you? Because something's the matter, something's bothering you, that's for sure."

"You already asked me that."

"I'm asking you again."

"You asked me hours ago." She signaled absurdly toward the mountain road the jeep was going up, as if the question were there, waiting for them "And I don't see how anything's changed. Nothing's bothering me, I already told you that."

"Okay, then nothing's the matter. I'm glad."

"Maybe something's bothering you? Let's see if you tell me. What's on your mind?"

"You really want to know?"

She smiled. "Yes, because you get so ugly when you're worrying, your skin gets all wrinkled, here and here." She caressed the skin around the corners of his mouth. "So if you tell me what you're thinking about, then I'll be able to know what it is just by looking at the wrinkles. You can't have any secrets. I'm going to know them all, every last one."

"You really want to know?"

"Yes."

"I was thinking about my home."

"Our home?"

He chose not to respond. With one arm he pointed toward the hills that were beginning to lose their green, the breeze no longer so cool as they left the valley's fertility. "Nothing's changed, it's incredible." He eased off on the gas pedal going into a curve. "I used to come here, as a kid, miles and miles, just to see a festival of green like this. I knew I couldn't come in. The owner wouldn't allow it and my father wouldn't have either. Even then it was all fenced off. Pity the kid who got caught in the orchards."

"Poor thing," she said. "But you picked plenty of fruit, didn't you?"

"Not one apple. Don't ask me why, but I felt that my duty, even then, was to protect the fruit, protect the owner's property. From the other side of the wire, I scared the birds away, that's what I did."

"You didn't take any fruit? What did you come for, then?"

"For the green. That's what. It was enough to look at the house's gardens from a distance, from a nearby hill. Even then I knew, I don't know how, but I knew it in my bones like I know there's God, like I know the two of us are here now, I looked at that green and calmed down, all my sadness and rage disappeared, I knew that some day I was going to have to get out of my house, out of my village. I knew that those rocks couldn't keep me prisoner forever. I knew I'd do anything to get away. Absolutely anything."

"And did you know you were going to do it with me?"

He looked at her now, amazed, tender. "You're going to laugh, but yes. I knew that too."

"We could go by and see your house. It isn't far from here, is it?"

"From the owner's house it's six hours on foot...but in the jeep we could do it in less than an hour."

"Six hours, on foot?"

"Every Sunday. I didn't care what they'd do to me when I got back. Every Sunday, before anybody was up, I was already on my way. Later my father would beat me. He gave it to me good. I got home at dusk and there he was, waiting. My sister told me once that Sundays, the first thing he'd do was go to my bed to see if I'd done it again, and then he'd sit there, by the door, all day, waiting for me to come back. Every Sunday. But it was worth it."

"Let's go," she said. "It's not late. I'd like so much to visit the house you were born in."

Emmanuel pressed down on the gas and the rough sound of the motor almost drowned out his reply, which came out in a kind of vicious whisper. "What for? There's nothing to see. A house like any other. Like yours in Longa. A shitty house."

"The place where you were born can't be the way you say it is. Come on, let's go."

"No. In a few years, maybe."

"When we come back from the city?"

"When we come back from the city?" he said, doubtfully. "Sure, maybe then."

Her voice sweetened. "You know what I'd like? I'd like to have known you when you were little. Really little."

"What for?" but Emmanuel smiled, the hostility draining from his body. For an instant, they both felt how his hand settled on her skirt, the thigh beneath. She took it in hers. He withdrew it reluctantly and set it back on the wheel.

"To take care of you, protect you. You cried, didn't you?"

"I never cried," he said abruptly. "Not even when I was born. If I told you... My mama says I yelled plenty but never a tear. I don't have any water in me. Nothing's ever been able to get a drop out of me. I think that's what made my old man so furious. Maybe that's why he hit me so hard."

"Poor little love."

"Poor? No way. I deserved it. I knew I wasn't supposed to make those trips. I had to pay the price. Nothing's free in this life. If they don't hand you the bill today, you'll get it tomorrow. You can count on that. If some kid of mine got mixed up with my enemies, I'd do the same thing."

"You'd do that to a child of ours?"

He suddenly hit the brakes. There was a little turnout at the side of the road, at the edge of a precipice. He shut off the motor and twisted around in the seat to face her. Behind her, the valley was dancing, green and rich, the leafy exuberance contrasted with that brown face, her dark, sad, sparkling eyes.

"We're in a war, Cecilia. Do you know what a war is?"

She shut her eyes. Without opening them, she answered, "I know something of what a war is, yes."

"You take sides and if you lose, you're fucked. I decided early on, the first time I saw this valley, the owner's land, that my old man was on the wrong side, he'd already lost. You know something? I didn't even decide that. Some part of me's always known it. That's why he didn't want me to come around here. None of the men in town should work for Philip Kastoria, he said. He said Kastoria's family had taken away land that was ours, by fraud and by force, who knows how many decades or centuries back. He knew that if I came here I'd fall in love with this land, that I'd end up enlisting with Philip Kastoria."

"And what did you say when that happened? Did you realize you had the right to choose?"

"I didn't say anything. I never said anything. One day I just didn't come back. I never saw him again. He must have stood there waiting for me by the door of the house with the strap ready and his eyes scanning the horizon. It was okay that he beat me. It was his duty. He already knew that I was the enemy, that I'd gone over to the other side. He could see it coming. And Mr. Kastoria knew it too. Men have a way of knowing these things. You can't understand. He'd scarcely laid eyes on me, the minute he saw me he must have known that here was somebody useful. I scared off the birds from behind the fence, without ever going inside. One Sunday the gates opened and out he rode on horseback, accompanied by his foreman. He came straight to where I was. He didn't even say hello. 'You want work, don't you, boy?' he asked me, in the same tone as I'm telling you. 'Yes, sir,' I told him. I didn't look down. I looked right at him. 'You're hired.' That's what he said to me, and before going on his way, I remember one more thing. You know what he said?"

"No." Something trembled in her voice.

"He said, 'You've got to shoot the birds that eat the fruit. That way they won't come back.' And that's when I knew I wasn't going home. I was fourteen. I haven't seen my father or my sisters once since that Sunday."

"Someone should have explained to your father that you were going to be important."

Emmanuel started the engine again. "Important? Who says I'm important?"

"I say so."

"Oh, all right. That's different."

"To the captain and others you're important, and I suppose to Mr. Kastoria."

"Important?" He gunned the jeep almost angrily onto the road.

"I would have known it right away. Even when you were little. That's something women can tell but you men can't."

"You like little kids a lot, don't you?"

"A lot. I'd like to have millions and millions of kids."

He smiled. "Millions is a bit much."

"Thousands, then. And they should all have your eyes."

"In the city you can't have as many kids as in the country. You know that, don't you?"

"Why not?"

But he didn't answer.

"Here we are," said Emmanuel, braking.

The orderly hoped his memory wouldn't fail him. He'd try not to leave out a single significant detail. He'd begun by greeting Beatrice Kastoria and the two men. They, for their part, had seemed particularly pleased to see him after all this time. It had been several months, actually, since he'd been to visit them. Since the change of command in the region. Beatrice Kastoria had asked him to sit down, despite the dust he brought in from the road, offering him a drink, which he declined. She had jokingly reproved him. Perhaps he was an ingrate who'd now grown distant from his former employers. He had responded that they weren't former, that he considered himself always at their service. They had been like parents to him when he—

"It's true I asked for details," complained the captain, "but you can skip the personal history."

The orderly thought that perhaps that part of the conversation might have interested the captain, since that's what made it possible to hear Philip Kastoria's opinions, and those of his family, concerning the current situation, which was the main part of his report.

The captain looked at him awhile without responding. He set about rolling a cigarette, morosely, thoughtfully. He looked out the window and spied the clear light of a moon coming out from behind the hills, a soft glow that scarcely reached them, and was annoyed by the strong aggressive glare of the bulb hanging over his desk.

Then he said, "Emmanuel"—it was the first time he had pronounced his name, that he hadn't addressed him formally—"tell me something. Were they really like parents to you?"

"Let's stop here," said Emmanuel.

"You said there wasn't time."

"I was wrong. We've got plenty of time. This place. I want you to know it."

It was the river. The same one. This high up in the mountains it sounded different, though, hadn't yet taken on the muddy tint that colored it miles below. But it was the same river, that water, he knew how it flowed, the way it ran over the rocks. Since he'd washed in it all his life, as far back as he could remember, since he'd come down here in search of the stray nanny goat, since he'd played his first games, since the first tales were spun, that river, that one, it was unmistakable.

He got out and waited for her to follow. But she stayed in the jeep, her eyes evasive, jittery, going over a limited but shifting space behind him, toward the shore.

Emmanuel came up to the window and put both arms on the door. "Come on." She didn't move. "Come on, do you hear."

"I don't want to."

"You don't want to?"

"Not here, no."

"Yes, here, right here," he said. "Come with me, I'm going to explain to you why this spot."

"Whatever you say." But she didn't move this time either.

Something mischievous flickered in Emmanuel's cheeks, something between fun and tender pride danced over his face. "Look, Cecilia, I'm telling you, don't worry about the river. It doesn't see anything. And if it does, it doesn't tell anyone. But the things it could tell."

He opened the door and took her by the hand. She didn't resist. She let him lead her, indifferent, secretive, enclosed in her own confused eyes. They walked over rocks, tripping, more or less at random, as if he'd collected all the will available, as if only he and the river really existed and she were nothing more than a pair of legs, a pair of arms, some bones that by chance happened to be here now, some burning ashen eyes that seemed the only thing alive in her woman's body pulled along by a man.

Were they really like parents to him? Perhaps it was a bit bold, sir, to put it that way, perhaps that was going a little too far. In light of the fact that it had come up in the conversation, well, he'd felt the need to report it like that, as it was. Nevertheless, since he'd been asked directly, he'd offer an opinion. Yes, in fact, the master and his wife Beatrice—given of course the distance between them and him, without his ever overstepping his position, without attributing too much importance to himself—had always treated him with consideration, with respect, and even, if the word didn't bother the captain, with affection. They had always encouraged him to overcome his ignorance, to perfect his knowledge of arithmetic. They'd suggested readings, they'd kept promoting him to positions of trust. Among the servants Mr. Kastoria had shown him off as evidence that all wasn't lost, so they might see an example of what can be done if one has the will. Finally, what more could a boy born a peasant desire than to have come to serve the most powerful man in the region and one of the most influential in the life of the province and perhaps the nation?

"That's fine," said the captain. "Loyalty is one of the bulwarks of our country. It's what holds everything else together. But I asked you for another reason. There's something else I'm interested in knowing."

The captain had only to speak. He was at his service.

"Without a family, Emmanuel, we're lost. We owe everything to our parents. Our birth, our education, our gratitude. But that's where conflicts can arise. Suppose, let's say, there were suddenly a conflict. Well, not necessarily a conflict, let's call it a misunderstanding, between your master and the army, who knows, a difference of opinion... It's a possibility, isn't that so?"

In the midst of all the rocks was just one tree, majestic, radiant, surrounded by little bushes that blocked the view from the road. They went to sit in that perfect enveloping sensuous shade. Emmanuel was right. Nobody ever came down this road. They were alone. The two of them. And the tree. And the river. It was like being in a house, or almost like that. Outside the sun beat down hatefully, shattering the air.

"How come you're so far away? Come over here."

She drew her body nearer to his. She looked at his hand placed lightly on her skirt, moving down playfully toward her knee which he could feel under it, then climbing again. She arranged his jacket against the thick rugged trunk of the tree and stared at the river.

"Now I'm not far away," she said.

He brought his lips to her hair, his fingers happily wandered over the tense cords of her throat, then reached inside her dress and played with her nipples. He repeated the operation, licking her ear, hoping for some reaction. He stopped next to her lips, touching her as if one of them were blind. Suddenly he said, "Something's wrong. Nobody's going to convince me that nothing's wrong. Isn't it time to tell me what it is?"

"I don't like this place, that's all. We'd better go. It's getting late."

He tried to catch her eye but she avoided his gaze, she kept looking at the river, fascinated by its swirling motion, its color, its sleepy rocky sound. There was nothing special about the river.

Then he decided to change positions, arranging his head in her lap where he could look up and study her face while they talked. He took one of her hands and ran it through his own hair.

She smiled timidly and mechanically began to work one lock that insisted on sticking up above the rest.

"You know why I like this place?"

She didn't answer.

"Hey, girl, Cecilia, I'm talking to you."

"Yes, my love."

"You weren't listening."

"You asked whether I knew why you like this place."

Above, beyond her body, her face, the tree's leaves were ablaze, dense sunlight filtering through. A bumblebee marked off the boundaries of the surrounding air, steadily buzzing and buzzing.

"Before, you know, I came here all the time."

"Before?"

"Before Kastoria asked me to go with Captain Gheorghakis. I used to come down here, alone. When I had a little free time. I walked along the bank of the river and you know what I did? I amused myself by throwing rocks. I could spend hours throwing rocks into the river. More and more, until there was nothing around me but a piece of bare ground. Then I'd move a few yards, and again more rocks, tossing them in. I could spend hours like that. When I was much younger I thought if I threw them in all day it was possible to fill up the riverbed, maybe even change its course."

"A dam? We tried to build a dam too."

"This was different. Because I wasn't putting the rocks in a single spot, I was just tossing them in to hear the sound. But one day I stopped. I realized two things." He waited, but she said nothing. "It was never going to happen. The river hadn't changed a bit. And the second thing was that even if I succeeded, it was pointless. Because then the only thing that would be accomplished was that the course of the river would be different, here along the shore where we are now, and then I'd have to start all over again, carting rocks from the new bank till the bed was filled, and so on forever. I never threw another rock into this river."

"Silly dear, the things my love thinks up," she said, but in her eyes he could see the dirty current of the river running toward Longa, toward a place that wasn't here.

"But I liked it for other reasons. I liked it because of you. Yes, you. I didn't come here alone, I was dreaming of you. With my eyes wide open, under this very tree. I sat myself down the same as now, with my hands behind my head, of course, since your pretty little lap wasn't here, and I set about calling you, sort of crying, calling to you. I could see your whole image outlined in the leaves, sketched from one point to another."

At that moment she might have said that that was impossible, he didn't even know her then, how could that be. He waited awhile for her to say something, noticing the rasping interruption of that bee buzzing nearby, then continued, "It wasn't any other girl. It was you. Even before I met you. I was always waiting for you. I was getting ready here, love. Love, I was waiting for you on this very spot. Right here. That's why I like this spot. Because here's where I needed you. And you were looking at the same river, far away. I...You're going to laugh, but I dared, that's the word, I dared to suppose you existed, that some day soon I was going to meet you. It was enough to want you here under this tree. It was enough to... Are you listening now?"

Now yes, she answered, just as she should have, "My poor little treasure, how lonesome he was," but the words didn't carry enough conviction. He could feel her playing a role to please him, her mind, her emotions, even her body someplace else, controlled by forces he couldn't know.

"It was like an empty space, here beside me, like a physical absence, a place you had to fill. I imagined your lap, and us here just like this, and you who would understand me. We talked. You know that? I talked to you and you answered and I wasn't afraid. There wouldn't be a single lie between us. We'd tell each other everything. We were going to go to the city, you'd go with me, it was already decided that as soon as you appeared, we'd go. That's where we'd have our children, in the city."

"Our children?" she asked in a distant, metallic sort of voice.

Playfully he caught the hand she kept untangling his hair with. He brought it to his mouth and whispered softly, feeling his breath enveloping, rebounding off that warm skin, "Yes," he said to her hand. "Our children in the city. Not here. I had it all planned out. You can't imagine how completely I was preparing every one of our acts. Even today's." He hoped her catlike curiosity would be kindled, that she'd repeat the words with mishievous innocence. Today's? and what are you thinking of doing today, you rascal, you nasty man, you silly child? But her hand only pulled away from his lips, went back to work in his hair, that was all that indicated she was there. He shut his eyes and let the shreds of sunlight speckle them, both of them rocked by the nearby rhythm of the river he couldn't control. "Even today's. We'd come here just one time, and never again after that. And you can see it now, we're here, in fact.

This is no dream. And you're no vision. Everything's coming true, exactly. Exactly."

He was going to go on, when he felt Cecilia's body stiffen. Her thighs had lost that special, sheltering softness. They were tense, trembling, hard. Even her hand went rigid. He knew he needed to open his eyes. Everything in her transmitted an urgency alien to what he was saying, to the enchanted situation. But he didn't want to. The drowsiness was so sweet. When he finally looked, something was definitely wrong. Something was happening to her and it wasn't just in her face, it wasn't just in her body. It was like one of those fun-house mirrors that twist and dismantle a person's image. With a hard, dark glare her eyes were rejecting what they saw, what they saw in the river, what she was seeing in spite of herself in the river.

"There," a voice stammered, it came from her throat but wasn't hers. "Over there."

With the captain's permission, the orderly didn't consider that a possibility at all, not even remotely. A conflict, large or small, between Philip Kastoria and the nation's armed forces was impossible. Their interests were completely identical. He saw himself obliged to inform the captain in advance that he didn't see himself serving two masters. He reminded him that, on the contrary, it was Philip Kastoria himself who provided his services to Captain Gheorghakis at the beginning of the struggle against the bandits, that he hadn't imposed conditions limiting those services, and that he had approved his continuing in that position, even when there'd been a change of command.

The captain got up and stretched his whole body, his tight muscles, then collapsed in his armchair. A couple of flies continued to circle senselessly around the light bulb. In the distance, in darkness, dogs barked.

"Look, Emmanuel. It's natural for the army to want to know the mettle each of its soldiers is made of. I'm not saying that you have to choose between anything. You'll probably never be faced with such a conflict. But out there, all of a sudden, who knows what turns life can take. For my part, I don't know what plans Kastoria has for you once this war is over. Perhaps it would be a good idea to tell him you're anxious to come with me to the city. Did you talk about that?"

They hadn't touched on the subject. The orderly knew that his job was always open, always available, that Mr. Kastoria would always need the services of men like him who were totally loyal. Besides, if it didn't offend the captain, sir, the orderly found the subject most unpleasant. He didn't like having to conceive of such a situation. Was it possible for him to proceed with his report.

"There," repeated the voice that wasn't hers. "There, over there."

He felt the panic beginning but shut it off by throwing a look in every direction, searching, searching the horizon. Crouching, staggering, he reached for his revolver.

"What?" he demanded, furious. "Where is it?"

But she was already running toward the river, falling between the rocks, slipping, insane, helping herself along with her hands, crawling on all fours, a crazy person, some crippled, terrified animal.

"Cecilia! Cecilia, wait!"

She paid no attention.

He threw a half look up at the road, turned to the violent flow of the river. There was nothing, nobody, not a thing. "Cecilia!"

Then he saw it too. It was something like a figure, a shape in the water, something vaguely floating in the muddy foam, something compact, ambiguous, probably human in the water. The thing, caught between fallen trees on the opposite bank, moved against the jagged end of the trunk in a way that was black and stained and heavy.

Cecilia was advancing toward the riverbank as if she were going to throw herself into the current.

"No!" he yelled again. "Wait!"

Since she seemed to hear nothing, since she seemed to be out of control, he cocked his gun and fired in the air. The shot echoed dryly between the hills. He was shocked by the sudden desperate fluttering of birds taking flight from the vegetation, as if someone had violated a truce, quarreling and squawking in the air in sudden angry confusion. But the shot worked. She'd stopped still, a motionless statute frozen halfway across the rocky beach.

"Don't move! It could be a trap, an ambush!"

Slowly he inched his way forward, his gun ready, steadily scanning the shadows of the bushes, the sharp angles of the stones behind which nobody could be hidden. When he reached her side, he saw she was pale and sweaty and cold, at the mercy of the thing floating on the other side of the river.

"It's him," said Cecilia. "It's him. I knew he'd come. I knew it. I told Mama. It's him."

"Stay here. You're not to move. Understand?"

Since she just kept muttering, it's him, it's him, it's him, in a very low toneless voice, her cheeks colorless, it's him, it's him, it's him, the moan of a wounded animal, Emmanuel decided to quickly cover the distance left between him and the boiling edge of the river. It looked bad. What seemed to be a dead man (or was it a woman, could it be a woman with some sort of shivering long hair, that flowing blackness?), the man was submerged in the water, and the tangled branches of the trees, a few leaves that still hadn't fallen or kept on growing stubbornly obstructed the clear identification of the form the waves were agitating, lifting, sinking, dashing against the rocks, hiding behind the foliage. Farther upriver the dirty mirror of the water reflected the sun's imperfect glare. Emmanuel shaded his eyes and tried to find a place where they could cross. He remembered a few round, flatish stones downriver. There they were. They could serve as a bridge.

"Come, Cecilia," he said smoothly, trying to smile. "Do you want to come with me? Shall we see what it's all about?"

She obeyed, a manikin. Only her eyes had any life, restless eyes, exhausted, teary. "Put that away," was all she asked, pointing weakly toward the gun, not turning her face in his direction, drawn by the bundle slowly twisting in the flow.

Now he had both hands free. He tried to put emphasis and certainty in his voice. "It's nothing. There's so much garbage in this river."

"It's him, it's him," Cecilia's floating, dark eyes repeated, but she herself didn't say a word. She accepted the hand he offered her. But he noticed her fingers were lifeless and she didn't respond to his squeeze.

The captain waited another instant, examining the figure of the orderly standing before his desk, and then blinked a couple of times as if swallowing air through his eyes.

"So, you gave my letter of invitation to Kastoria?"

He had taken the liberty of including Mr. Kastoria's brother Sebastian in the invitation, since if the captain had known of his presence, his visit, he undoubtedly would have wanted him to attend the dinner in honor of Colonel von Spand.

"Fine. And the brother, is he coming?"

Unfortunately, he had to return to the capital in a few days. Because of that, he wouldn't be in the area next week. Nevertheless, he sent his regards.

"But Kastoria is."

Yes, of course. He was nonetheless uneasy about what he called the business of the river. He wanted more details. How long was that going to last? Those had been his words.

"Repeat them to me exactly."

And how long is that going to last? That was how Mr. Kastoria put it. And he added, I see that your captain has a soft hand, fuck it all.

"He said that, in those words?"

With your permission, sir, that's what he said.

"And how did you answer him?"

He had indicated that the captain's patience was running short, that the captain was acting under orders not to provoke an irreversible confrontation with the populace, and, finally, that the captain had indicated to the lieutenant that the affair was going to be cleaned up, one way or another, before the German colonel arrived.

"That's what you told him?"

Yes, sir, that's what he'd told him.

During the brief crossing, he sensed she was calming down. They had to pay close attention to their feet, concentrate on every rock, stay aware of the powerful flow of the river, think about the next rock, and the next, and take care not to fall, they had to feel the strength of the tendons and muscles anchoring them to every little island along the way. They had to work together with their hands and arms and shoulders and the trembling of their bodies, their shoes spattered with foam. They had to avoid looking upriver, toward the trees and that thing bobbing and sinking, always trying to keep their balance.

When they reached the other shore, they let their eyes, which had been looking down, go on ahead, examining the path they'd now have to find. At last their legs guessed where to stop, near the rotting roots of the two big trees, and then he raised his eyes and swung his gaze suddenly toward the river. He reached for a branch and began twisting it furiously until a long dry crooked stick was left in his hands.

"Don't move."

She watched him advancing out on one of the trunks, progressing very carefully toward the end. Near the tip she saw him stop, holding onto one of the branches, balancing against the current. She wanted to tell him to be careful, but nothing came out. Her mouth felt full of dust. Then she saw him using the stick like a shovel, like he was poking a fire. The shape insisted on turning over every time the stick touched it. She wanted to shut her eyes, but the air or the light or the river kept them wide open. Something forced her to focus on Emmanuel in the fallen trees, the rush of the river racing like her heartbeat into the valley below, the body responding to every savage shove of the stick.

Then Emmanuel turned around.

"Look," he shouted over the noise of the river. And she could read an unreal grin on his face. "Look, it's nothing." And on the point of the stick hung an old black washed-out raggedy piece of cloth, once a dress or a curtain or shroud, now nothing but a stinking, dripping hunk of rag.

"Who is it?" she asked, not wanting to understand.

"Nobody. It's nobody. Just a piece of shit. A shitty rag."

And he threw the stick toward the shore. It fell at Cecilia's feet. She stepped back, trying to fathom the water spilling from that dead corroded branch.

"What did I tell you?" Emmanuel came back quickly along the trunk, talking nonstop, triumphantly. "Just nerves. We've been poisoned by so many stories. Didn't I tell you? Didn't I say this river's full of garbage?"

He came up to her, lifted the stick again, and swung it around in the air, spattering them with mud. He swung it as if there were a garland on the end of it or a trophy of war or an enemy's head.

"Didn't I tell you it was all nonsense? Didn't I tell you?" He waited for her to make some comment and then added, "My captain always says that we have to watch out for the living. That the dead watch out for themselves. So let's quit kidding ourselves about these old wives' stories. Stories of old bitches who don't know anything about anything. Ignorant old bitches."

As her only response, she took his arm and lowered it. Then she caught hold of the stick and, pulling, dropped it on the ground. There it stayed. Then she pulled his hand toward her heart and placed it there. He could feel that pounding under her smooth skin. A fish flopping around about to die, about to burst, explode.

"Did you really think it was your..."

"Yes," she said. "It was him. I thought it was him."

His hand moved down, lightly touching her breast, it was the beginning of a soft massage, undulant, musical, warm. He reached around with his other hand and pulled her to him.

"But it wasn't."

"No," she said. "It wasn't."

"Do you want to stay here? Or shall we go back to the other side?"

"Whatever you say, love," she answered.

"Let's go back over, to my tree. Come on."

"Whatever you say," she repeated.

Then Mr. Kastoria's brother had wanted more details, so he had felt obliged to tell him the whole story, including Sofia Angelos's recent decision to camp by the river and the subsequent agitation all over the region. His brother had commented, in light of this, that these affairs should be cleared up with a good round of bullets and that it was a shame there was always some guy who thought himself very intelligent and counseled the army badly, obstructing its proper work. On his return to the capital he was going to speak with military friends of his and advise them once and for all that it was about time to do something. Where else in the world do illiterate peasant women hold the nation's armed forces in check? What we conquered by force they now wanted to take away from us with negotiations and empty words about national reconciliation.

"Why are you stopping? Go on."

The problem is that just then Mrs. Kastoria intervened.

"Beatrice?"

Yes, sir, that's right. She didn't ordinarily participate, but she'd gotten quite visibly agitated since he'd begun telling the story, and suddenly she spoke up. She wanted to say that she understood those poor women, and that really it was time to return their husbands to them if the army had them or knew where they were, and besides, she thought that the captain had acted with considerable prudence, with great care and even with wisdom, if such praise didn't embarrass the captain, but as far as he could remember, that's how she'd expressed it. And that it was good to count on soldiers who harbored healthy sentiments and who did all they could to find nonviolent solutions to problems. She hoped everything would turn out peacefully, because there had already been too much bloodshed and vengeance, and that she was tired and fearful, and that her brother-in-law would do well to exhort his friends not to force things. She and Philip had to go on living in the country, while he was happy in the city and wouldn't suffer the consequences.

"What did her brother-in-law say to that?"

Nothing, sir, because Mr. Kastoria took over. He indicated to his wife that she understood nothing of political matters, that she shouldn't get involved, that she should leave this business to men. Then he tried to coax her into saying what she was afraid of.

"And she?"

She said, after a bit of wheedling, that she'd heard rumors, she knew of bodies that had started turning up everywhere, even in their private fields and orchards, right on their property they were appearing, perhaps hanged, dead men, and that those dismembered men, they started walking around at night, all rotting and dirty and faceless, and nothing could stop them, because nothing can stop the dead, and that the servants whispered of nothing but that, and the farm hands too, and even the guards. And that she'd awakened the other night in a sweat and gone down and found the doors open, the doors of the house, someone had left the doors wide open, and that one of those dead men could have come in, someone had left the doors open for just that purpose, someone.

With the captain's permission, it was pitiful to see Mrs. Kastoria so upset, because she had always been a model of serenity, a truly sweet woman. He'd have the chance to meet her at the dinner.

"Women are sweet, that's true. Sweet and unforgettable. But they wouldn't exactly make model soldiers, would they?"

No, the captain was absolutely right. All of them, all of them let themselves be influenced by this kind of foolishness.

"Then what happened?"

Philip Kastoria intervened again, first to calm her down, then to confirm that the situation was becoming impossible, that it was good the visit of Colonel von Spand would put things in order. That that was very, very good. That it was sad to admit that the Germans had to force our own soldiers—among whom was no one more nor less than the son of General Constantopoulos, those were Philip Kastoria's words, so the captain would understand them as such—our own soldiers, he said, to show more balls. Or did the captain prefer that he, Kastoria, and his men should impose a little order? Otherwise the foreign colonel would do it in his own way. But that it was preferable for our army to take care of our own internal affairs, our own problems, it was about time.

"And did he say anything else?"

Yes, sir, that we should take care of business, and he added, if they can. That.

"If they can? He said that?"

More or less that. It was hard to repeat it word for word. But that was the sense of it.

"And you, what did you say to him then?"

He hadn't said anything. He didn't even know what immediate plans the officers had.

"What we're going to do, you'll see soon enough. And that old bitch, she's going to see too."

"I don't want him to be born here," said Emmanuel. "Not here."

She didn't answer. She let fall one of the little stones she had in her hands, followed its playful roll with her eyes, picked it up to hold it, let it go, picked it up again, over and over. He studied her game. Suddenly he reached, stretched, intercepted the stone.

"Give me my pebble," she sang. "It's mine, give it to me."

Emmanuel hesitated. He opened his fingers provocatively, so they could both see its shiny black-and-white design, then shut his fist again.

"Who says it's yours? Prove it to me."

"It's mine," she said stubbornly. "You're stronger, but it's mine. I was playing with it."

"Come take it from me then," Emmanuel's eyes sparkled. "Or give me something for it. Let's see, what can you give me?"

She leaped and tried to catch his hand in the air, but he easily evaded her.

"I shouldn't have to give you anything, but all right, to avoid problems, to make peace, I'll offer you a kiss. No, five kisses. One for each finger. No, no, six, one for each finger and another for the palm of your hand."

"This is a very valuable pebble. Very magical. It takes away all your troubles, every single one, and it's the stone of truth, besides."

She grabbed hold of his arm. With one hand she was artfully reaching down toward his fist, sneakily advancing like a centipede.

"The stone of truth?"

"Yes. Whoever holds it has to tell the truth, can't help it, when someone asks him a question. And even more so if it's a woman."

"That's not so. It's a lie."

She'd reached his fingers and was trying to pry them loose. When she managed to get one free, she went to work on the next one, but he took advantage of her concentration, as intense as a child's, to close the first one again.

He grinned with a festive innocence.

"I'll give it to you, you know. But when you have it you have to take very good care of it."

"Better than you. That little pebble wants to roll. It wants to be dropped and picked up again. It wants a pretty hand like mine. Look how pretty it is. Not an ugly one like yours that'll hurt it, keep it shut up all day—no sunlight, no nice little lizards."

"You have to answer one question, that's all. When I give it back, okay?"

"Okay," she said. "If I can."

"I'm going to whisper it, like this, real slow, in your ear, so just you and the little pebble and me can hear."

"Give it to me."

"Promise?"

"Of course." Suddenly her voice was serious. "Besides, I don't have any secrets. There's nothing about me that you can't know."

"Then here's the pebble."

Her face lit up. She felt the pebble, polished it with her breath, rubbed it along her arm to feel its clean smoothness. "It's mine. It's mine and I'm never going to let go of it."

He came closer. "I'll collect the six kisses later," he said. "Now for the question."

She arched her neck so her head was right next to Emmanuel's mouth.

"Do you have the pebble?" he asked in a murmur she barely heard over the river rattling through the stones. She nodded and showed her little fist which had closed around the tiny treasure.

"Then you have to tell me the truth." She nodded once more. He felt how her body softened, melted into his. "Remember, this stone is the stone of truth." Again she nodded yes. "Tell me, then"—and he lowered his voice until it could barely, just barely be heard—"are you pregnant?"

"And that's all? You haven't forgotten anything?"

No, sir. That was all. Perhaps the captain needed something else? Perhaps he had some other question? Because if not, sir, he'd excuse himself.

"No, thanks. I don't need anything."

Then the orderly wanted to take the opportunity to thank the captain for his kindness in letting him take his girl friend on this trip. It was a gesture he appreciated, he wouldn't forget it, if it wasn't presumptuous of him to say so.

"It's nothing."

The captain watched him heading for the door and concealed a vague smile. "Oh yes, one more thing."

Whatever the captain says, sir.

"Did you tell Kastoria that I'd offered to help you go to the city?"

The captain should forgive him, but he didn't understand the question.

"Did you tell Kastoria that soon it was likely you'd be returning with me to the capital? Did you tell him that?"

With his permission, it didn't seem appropriate that he should discuss with Mr. Kastoria his private conversations with his military superiors.

In the silence, the barking dogs could be heard, the dogs on the hill barking for the moon behind the clouds. The captain took advantage of the pause to observe the orderly there by the door. He let another second go by, drumming his fingers on the desk top, then put both hands behind his neck.

"So you'd say it was a satisfactory visit, all the way around?"

Yes, sir. He believed that the visit had accomplished all its intended objectives. He could assert, since he was being asked, that without a doubt the trip had been more than satisfactory. Much more.

She dropped the pebble.

"You are," she said, and though her body didn't change, her voice spat it out, "a pig. A pig."

"You didn't answer the question."

"The answer is no." And now she scrambled away from him and looked back in a rage. "No. And no. And no again. I'm not pregnant. I'm not expecting any baby. Not yours or anyone's. Are you happy now? Now are you satisfied? You want to go off with another woman now? You want to? Is that what you want?"

"Silly girl. You're jealous. It was a game, that's all. Nothing but a game."

"Pig, pig. Our baby's not a game."

He tried to approach her but she backed away. She stopped at the edge of the tree's shadow.

"I didn't know what was wrong with you, love. You were acting so strange. I thought that was why."

"Well, that wasn't why. Are you happy now?"

"Yes, very happy. I don't want him to be born here."

"Couldn't you have asked me in a different way, directly, with trust, like we've always done? You don't trust me anymore, do you."

Something hardened in Emmanuel's tone. "I told you I didn't want him to be born here. That's all. I thought that was why you were acting strange."

"I'm not acting strange," she said.

He got up, brushing his pants off with his hand. "Fine. You're right. You're not. But then, what's wrong with you? Will you tell me what in hell's going on in your head?"

"Nothing's going on in my head," said Cecilia, watching the river that kept on flowing into the valley where she had been born. "Absolutely nothing."

But she didn't pick up the pebble.

⊰ x ⊱

[My father had indicated here the existence of a section in the original manuscript, coinciding with the above number. As there seems, in fact, to be a gap at this point in the text, it's preferable to advise the reader of this omission. There is no way of knowing what might have happened or what was planned for this section of the novel.]

chapter seven

⸾ xi ⸾

Before they take the hood off, well before that, Alexis already knows where he is, he remembered this place.

You know those stairs where you stumble, this damp air that smells of shit, the harsh sound of footsteps along this endless stone corridor. They pull the hood off, and your eyes try to adjust to what ought to be darkness, they try to recognize the cell they'll see, that they've already seen once before.

"Light, goddamn it," orders the voice. Someone flicks a switch, a bulb lights up. This sudden blaze blinds you and leaves your retinas white with pain. Your eyelids shut involuntarily. Patiently, focusing your attention on something else, on the pain in your lacerated shoulder, you wait for the circles of fiery color to subside.

Again, the voice and soldiers pushing suddenly from behind. The automatic gesture of your hands is useless. You can't protect yourself. They're tied behind your back. That shoulder, the bad one, bangs against something, hard, long. Bars, it's the bars. Now the burning begins, your shoulder begins to burn.

"All right, woman, let's see if your tongue loosens up enough to say good-bye to your grandson. We've brought him here."

Beyond where the bars come together, leaning, resting against them, you can hear laborious movements approaching. You suppose it's her. Then, your grandma's voice, husky, grave, worried.

"The boy, Captain?"

"Boy? What boy? He doesn't look much like a boy to me. He's big enough to know how to go into hiding. We went looking a week ago, a whole week and it's only now we've managed to find this...boy."

Now you feel Grandma's hand. It starts on your hair, your cheek, goes down along your neck, as if it were she whose eyes were sub-merged, a blind woman confirming your features. That hand is remarkably hot and bony, and it stops there, gently massaging your neck muscles.

"What good can a boy do you, Captain?"

It isn't too hard to imagine the captain smiling, his mouth stretched tense, his teeth barely showing with every sentence, the upper lip twisted.

"What good can he do us? He can do a lot. To start with, we've got you talking. He's almost a miracle, this...boy. It's the first time we've managed to get a peep out of you, woman, and that's something already."

"So I'm talking, Mr. Captain, here I am."

Grandma's hand goes back up into your hair, then down to your neck, the nape, with a different rhythm, far from her voice, exploring, rocking, humming, with an urgency her voice doesn't have, feeling your ear, going around it, and again down the clean slope of your neck. Your eyes open, and despite the light's poisonous immediacy, they begin to distinguish your grandma's face close by, her eyes shining and near and heavenly with hunger, the cell behind her lightless.

"Tell your grandma why we're going to send you to the capital—hey—we told you before, did you forget already?"

what's grandma whispering with her hand. what would be blowing into your ear, spilling into you, if her words could get to you through some secret tunnel, like sap through a tree trunk, like a stream through a hollow, what whispered advice? that you speak as little as possible, child, she'd start with that. that you keep to yourself half, more than half, of what you're thinking. and that's why she dared to talk to the captain? she wasn't afraid? because what she was thinking, child, was infinitely worse. you mustn't forget there are several things they can't do, many things, many: one of them is to read our minds.

and the fear?

All of a sudden the hand comes down like a claw, the captain's hand, right on the screamingly painful shoulder, and yanks you backward. You almost fall, but with an effort keep your feet.

Grandma's hand stays where it was, like a wren frozen in the air, a few inches off. She sees that the captain is looking at her hand, capturing it with his cold eyes, and then she slowly withdraws the hand, grabs hold of one of the bars.

"You forgot already what boys your age are good for in the city? We just explained it to you and you forgot already?"

The pressure on your shoulder is becoming unbearable.

"I'm talking to you, punk. Didn't they ever teach you to answer when somebody asks a question?"

You focus your attention on Grandma and don't say a word. Can she know, can she tell, how much that shoulder hurts?

"Captain," says Grandma, "what do you want me to do?"

"Advise the women to go back home. The ones in your family and the others. We don't want to resort to force, Mrs. Angelos. You can bear witness to the goodwill of the nation's army. But our patience has a limit. In exactly six hours, at dawn, we're going to move them out of there...with arms if necessary. They're better off going on their own, and that way the boy goes free. You have my word of honor."

Her voice isn't trembling when she asks; "And if not?"

"Outside there are two army trucks..." The captain's fingers dig into your shoulder, stressing each word with a bitter, crippling clench. He doesn't even know, he can't know, has no way of knowing that you can feel those fingers all the way down your back, all the way along that shoulder you dislocated trying to get away, those tong-like fingers maiming your bones. You have to clench your teeth and bite hard and think your shoulder belongs to someone else, that all this is happening to somebody else's body, far away and getting farther. "Tomorrow morning one of them leaves for the capital. Your grandson is going to be on that truck as sure as there's a God. The other one leaves day after tomorrow, and you can guess who we're going to put on that one."

Grandma comes still closer to the bars. He almost has the impression she's going to go through the iron, going to turn herself into a shadow and pounce on the captain. Her body sticks there, furious, powerful, as if driven by a strong wind. But her voice isn't hostile or aggressive.

"Captain, do you have children, Captain?"

"What kind of question is that? Or are you threatening my family? Are you threatening my family?"

Grandma's voice grows even softer, hoarsening with emotion. It's been years since you heard her like this. You search your memory, but you may never have heard her like this before. Maybe to put you to sleep some night when Mama or Papa weren't there, maybe so you and Fidelia would sleep. Maybe.

"I'm not threatening anyone, Captain, who could I threaten? I was going to ask you a favor, in the name of your children. That's all."

"A favor?"

Now yes, inexplicably, the rage disappears from that voice and now yes, now yes, his hand lets go of your shoulder. For a second it's impossible to believe the relief flowing from your shoulder, that the commotion in your shoulder is easing, calming down.

He stands up straight, clears his throat, arranges his uniform. "Since you've mentioned my children, ma'am, and invoke them, go ahead, ask what you will. I hope I can satisfy you."

"Captain, tomorrow you'll be taking Alexis away. That's already decided. I can do nothing, sir, to prevent it."

You start to feel your heart beating, beating hard and rhythmically and mad, under your skin is the muffled shaking of what must be your own heart, which everyone must hear by now, a banging that can't be stopped. There's nothing Grandma can do to prevent what will happen tomorrow, nothing, nothing, there's nothing she can do, thoughts you have no way of canceling.

"You're refusing to cooperate, then. Are you refusing?"

She goes on as if she hadn't been interrupted. "All I can do, therefore, is ask you for a few hours, so we can say good-bye to each other. It isn't much to ask for, Captain."

Agitated breathing in the captain's chest, and the words boiling out. "So you're not going to go to the river? You're not going to cooperate?"

"There are things I should talk to my grandson about, Captain. A few hours, it isn't much."

a few hours, grandma? things to talk about?

until they've heard those footsteps, the old woman and the boy, those footsteps fading, leaving them alone, they won't attempt to speak. you're going to look at her serenely, not touching her, not yet hugging her, simply lingering in the quiet nocturnal company of one another, entranced by the growing silence, enjoying it and the darkness which shelters and protects them, and the absence of the soldiers, enjoying even the echo of the echo of those footsteps, until the echo's gone. she'll speak first, that's certain, before they come closer and touch, she first.

alexis?

yes, grandma.

alexis, she wasn't going to come back from the capital. you'll blink briefly, then a timid smile, quick, that she can't see. you'll take a step toward her, your arms extended, grandma, you...

no, alexis, she knew it, this is one thing she knew for certain. but she also knew for certain that he would. you are going to come back, alexis.

maybe, grandma, and then they'd embrace. there was no time to lose. any minute now the captain could return in a hurry to take these last few seconds from them, any minute the soldiers.

"And you," asks the captain, "what will you give me for this favor? What do I get out of it?"

"A bit of tranquility, Captain. Does that seem so little to you?" She's talking to him, but the calm in her voice is for you, as if she could protect you, steady your heartbeat, make that pounding take off forever, so the banging of your heart might subside like wings, so the soldiers at your back wouldn't know where the sound came from, so the captain, so that she herself and you, so no one in the world, and so no one could know what you're thinking and you don't want to keep thinking and aren't going to think.

"Something more substantial, Mrs. Angelos, more tangible. I believe in what I can touch. All right. I give you the kid for a few hours, what do you give me?"

"Captain, you've taken me from the river by force. I couldn't become your messenger now. The other women wouldn't take it well. And you know that already. I have nothing else to offer you."

"The truth is, really, that you never cease to amaze me. Gheorghakis told me, but I never believed it. You have an inexhaustible capacity to surprise me. Tell me something, there's something I'd like to know, out of sheer curiosity. What have you gotten out of all this? Have you got anything, one positive thing, out of this whole mess? One thing?"

Grandma looks at you when she speaks, not at him. The look goes into you and stays, very clear, very open, these words that can't be addressed to you the only ones she'll be able to say to you, the captain a pretext, a piece of wall. There could be something like the transparency of a smile on your grandma's lips, expanding these seconds, keeping the clock from ticking off time, this scarce short miserable time to go on being together.

"My men, Captain," Grandma pronounces severely, accenting every syllable. "And Captain, if you let me go, do you know what I'll do?" He doesn't answer. "I'll do it all over again, Captain. Everything. I don't regret a thing."

grandma?

yes, alexis.

did she really believe what she'd said to the captain?

what?

that we'd done everything right, that we'd do it all again if we had the chance?

maybe, alexis, it would be better if he were to give his opinion. did he believe they'd done the right thing? tell the truth, go ahead.

the truth is, not so good, grandma.

you'll feel the fatigue in her body, the way it's suddenly she who's resting her body on yours, it's she who is now in need. you're right, you hear her say, you suppose you will hear her say. she will admit it, and then she'd take a step back and you'd miss those skinny and bony and warm arms. but what choice did we have, alexis?

i don't know, grandma.

but someday he'd know, isn't that so? someday?

yes, grandma, i hope so, someday.

"She doesn't regret a thing," the captain says, shaking his head. He looks at the two soldiers, then at you, looking for some invisible interlocutor, some company. The soldiers exchange slight and cautious grins. "She doesn't regret a thing," repeats the captain. "This country's hopeless. They'll have to depopulate it and bring in other people, people from outside, people with some other kind of mind. With this race, there's no way, there's no place."

The captain makes a peremptory gesture, as if to leave. The soldiers react immediately. You feel the cord cut into you like a whip. Your grandma doesn't take her eyes off your face.

"And if I were your own wife, Captain, wouldn't you be content with her, wouldn't you ask her to do the same?" The words crawl out quickly, Grandma stopping time, Grandma looking at you.

The captain slowly lowers his hand. The cord loosens accordingly.

"You insist on mixing my family up in this. Nevertheless, I'm glad you ask. You know what I'd say to my wife? I'd tell her not to endanger the health of my children for anything in the world. Or my grandchildren, if I had any. War is men's business, isn't that right, Alexis?"

You don't say a word.

"A woman's place is in the home. Or in bed. That's where women belong, madam. Or don't they, soldier?"

One of the soldiers gives a nervous laugh, the other nods his head enthusiastically yes. They don't know what to do, what to say.

"All right, then, enough of this bullshit. Let's go."

Your body tenses, anticipating the blow on your shoulder, the cord cutting into your wrists. Your grandma keeps on looking at you, as if you were already up on the truck, as if you were up there and they'd started the motor.

"Captain," your grandma tries one last time. "We want very little. Just two things. Take care of them, Captain, and everything will work out."

The captain gives a signal and the soldiers stop, right behind you, you can feel those hands so close, a few inches, like eagle talons, ready.

"Let's hear the first one."

"Give us back the bodies of our men. That's the first thing we want."

what would he have done, grandma? to begin with, never that. never. it was wrong to say that papa and the rest were dead. he wouldn't accept that till he saw it with his own eyes, grandma, and even then he wouldn't believe it, he'd never believe it.

so he believed dimitriou was alive, is that right, alexis?

in the capital i'm going to find him, grandma. i'm going to look for him every place they take me. i'm going to ask every prisoner.

like serguei? and if they answered like serguei, child? mistakes, grandma, more mistakes. uncle serguei couldn't be treated like that. as long as she was asking him for the truth, why judge people that way?

then in the darkness you'd notice grandma straightening herself into a powerful posture, you'll feel her body turning hard again, only her skeleton there, her skin and flesh and guts and brains lifted off, shaded out, spirited away, a sheer invulnerable shadow, grandma. if we start to forgive, alexis, if we start justifying, we'll end by forgetting our own strength, we'll fall apart, we'll lose sight of the difference between right and wrong. in times like these that's how things were. and you as firm as she, with your pair of full-grown legs on the ground. no, grandma, in just these kinds of times you had to know how to forgive, you had to give a hand to those who were weaker than you.

forgive? the important thing was to survive. that was the key word, survive, did he understand?

now you can feel the night going away, you pick up the sounds that say the night is slowly draining off, that before long birds will be pushing the sun up, light filtering through the grating of the cell, the heat starting up again, soldiers' footsteps in the corridor and a truck waiting outside. so it was better to speak of papa, of grandma's youth, of mama's wedding dress, better the first time grandma saw alexandra at that dance, the first words babbled by fidelia, you'd ask her about those memories that only she has now, the time grandpa michael found himself alone in a tavern full of the landowner's thugs and his friend theodoro came in howling with joy, you had to hold every breath in the memory as the night moves on. whatever they do, you're not going to harden so much that you won't know how to forgive the fallen.

maybe, alexis, that's what she hoped.

"So that's the first thing. You don't want them alive anymore? Only dead?"

You catch the captain's neck muscles tightening, you sense a rumbling beginning in his throat which he keeps down and doesn't unleash, and in his stomach, and still lower, you see through those veins on the verge of bursting and his clenched teeth clenching and can tell that he too knows how to swallow his rage, store it up, feed it, winding and folding it in on itself, not offering it to anyone, the enemy also knows how.

but papa was alive, grandma, and if she declared him dead, they might really kill him someplace, in some jail. he wasn't going to contradict her in public, because these were family matters, and she knew where dirty clothes should be washed, but dead, grandma, not that.

"They're dead, Captain. We knew it as soon as my son walked through the doors of the school."

"And the second thing?"

it wasn't easy to come back home from where he would be, child, but she was going to tell him a few secrets, a few tricks, like a magician, alexis, little things that could help. suddenly you feel yourself a child again, you and fidelia, it makes you want to put your head in grandma's lap, right here and now, but you remain standing, like a grown-up, standing, hearing the night running out. you'll wait. grandma has never been the one to tell you stories. she didn't have time, she said. let the men take care of the children, let them help out with something at least. but now, for a while, her voice tempering the darkness, you can imagine nights that never were, around the fire or the kitchen in winter, or perhaps the way papa would have dreamed them when he was little. like serguei and cristina and rosa and maria, like maybe grandma herself had planned and envisioned it curled up at the foot of her mother or father or grandpa or in her youth or some glorious period of engagement, when we say we'll never change, we'll always know what it means to be young. of course later people forget, maybe out of the future like some terrible wave we feel coming, from so much anticipating the tragedy, from submerging ourselves in it, from knowing that cellars like these await us, that captains with that look, that bodies like those of your grandpa or your papa, and the river, and serguei coming back bowed and pale and a living insult to everyone, from so much, from so much that after a while one forgets how to celebrate the present, breathe in the moment, wash off your grief and bless the bread, and then one day it's like we'll have woken up and the moment will be gone, the pleasure vanished, we're here, alexis, waiting for those footsteps to take you away, unable to save you, without having told you any of this before, a grandma like a capped well, without having laughed together, and the day after tomorrow they'd take her away too, that's how we'd lived, like that.

except papa.

except dimitriou, dimitriou never had. our own sadness is enough, he would say, why add more?

that's why he was going to find him, grandma, in the capital i'm going to.

it could be, alexis, so listen closely, because she wasn't going to be coming back for sure, so listen.

"The second thing is that we want the killers punished, Captain."

There's disbelief, almost malice in the captain's voice. "You want the killers punished?"

"There was a crime, wasn't there? Then there has to be an investigation."

you suddenly hope that grandma will take out a potion that can turn you both invisible, herbs to make you evaporate, or something as practical and simple as a key capable of opening one door after another, a secret that can save you.

a secret, listen, little fool, another sort of secret. very simple. human beings are never alone. at the worst moment it was a matter of folding oneself inward and there he, you, whoever, would find something which, well, one carried the people you love inside, that's the truth. and that was all. if there was love, those people were inside you. these military men seem to see us, very defenseless, helpless. but one should feel sorry for them, finally, because they were so blind that they were shut off from their own insides, cut off. was that the secret, grandma, that?

"Well, woman, it's like I've said all along. This is nothing more than a political conspiracy."

"A conspiracy, Captain? My husband never even wanted me mixed up in politics."

"Politics, pure politics. They lost the war, and now they want investigations and trials. Mrs. Angelos, they're using you, and the worst thing about it is that you don't realize it, I believe you're completely unaware of it. Punish the killers? Impossible."

yes, that was the secret. you had to focus on a person. like when you were little and you wanted something deep down, even with your fingertips. it could be more, but one was enough. did he have someone he could, some person he could fix in his own mind? not let himself ever be separated from that person, always feel their presence, and when you speak it's as if they were listening and also were there in your mouth. and nothing you could say would make them feel ashamed. then you're never left alone. that's how. that's how one survives, talking with someone inside, that's how, she'll say, grandma will say, that's how. did he have some such person?

you'll close your eyes so the gray beginning of light now scarcely profiling grandma's face, the cot back there, the bars behind you, you'll close your eyes but you're not going to weaken and you're not going to give up even a teardrop.

yes, grandma, of course.

yes, of course, you little ruffian. you weren't telling your grandma, eh? you'll let her stroke your hair, she'll pull you roughly against her breast and pass that hand over your hair. then, then he'd come back. you can be sure, alexis, that if you have at least one person planted inside you, solid, growing, you'll make it back.

"Impossible? I don't think so, Captain."

you feel the footsteps, a ways off, on the stairs like a drowsy dripping which advances and starts to echo. you'll feel the unmistakable sound of footsteps coming with the first light, just before dawn.

and you, grandma, don't you have anyone inside to help you come back?

you'll see on her face the beginning, yes, it's definitely the beginning of a smile. the light's coming in and it's enough to make out subtleties, shades, her face. ah, child, she was full, stuffed, totally swollen with people. and if not, how, how could she have gotten through these years, but when one was old...the important thing is, was, that the people we've carried inside us find another home, they mustn't die out, alexis, understand?

yes, grandma, he understood.

The captain's voice shatters the scene with its urgency, surprising them both.

"Mrs. Angelos! Did you know that the day after tomorrow a German colonel is coming through here on a tour of inspection? Did you know that if I don't impose order, he will? Someone will always do it if I don't, there's no doubt about that. And I truly believe that if they decide to take charge of this region, you're going to be yelling out loud for my return. You'll remember me as the very Garden of Eden."

now no one can stop the approaching footsteps, those boots, those soldiers. you try to keep the anguish from choking your voice and you think you've managed to do it. you'll be speaking as casually as if you were home, under the tree, with fidelia nearby and mama and with...

the steps have arrived at the cell. hands are struggling with keys to open the door.

and they, grandma, how come they were so strong, his voice serene as if all the time in the world were before him, and not that deafening noise of keys and a door on the verge of opening and hands on the verge of, tell him that, how come they had so much, so much power, their enemies?

strong? her reply will arrive as if you were separated, as if an ocean already divided you or a mountain range or something worse. you think they're strong, alexis? take a good look at the difference between them and us. the difference. not so much that they were rich and we were poor or that they were armed and we defenseless or that they owned everything and we, well, we...but that they were empty, empty, understand, and we...it's clear how we are. they're empty, if you opened them a little sad blood might spill out and filth and after a while even their guts would disappear too, and that's why when they died, they died forever while

"And why are you explaining all this to me, Captain?" says Grandma's hardened, furious, contemptuous voice. "What for?"

and that's why when they died, they died forever, while we

"As a matter of fact," answers the captain, "you're absolutely right. What for?" And again he makes that gesture with his hand, this time yes, definitely.

"Just a minute, sir." You see how she reaches out now to touch you. Without even realizing it, you've been imperceptibly moving your body like a magnet toward the bars, slowly sliding toward her, and now her hand is fused with your arm. "Captain, you are better than that Gheorghakis. Captain, listen to me. They're going to go on appearing, one by one. You see already, Captain, how the river's been bringing them home. Until they've all come back. We're going to get them all, Captain, every single one. Be a good man, Captain. Why not bring them back yourself?"

The captain presses himself as close to the grate as he can. He's that close to Grandma and her outstretched arm, that close, but he doesn't touch her.

"You're not going to scare me with ghosts. I'm going to leave here and I'm going to have a good sleep and tomorrow morning I'm going to do my duty. And this conversation, this conversation never took place. I'm erasing it just like that. Nobody's going to remember it. Because you people, you people don't count. You don't count, understand? Look what all your efforts have accomplished. Look at this. Look."

And he makes a violent signal with his head, like a lion roaring, decisive, final.

You feel the thick hands pulling you. You try to take a step forward but the screaming in your shoulder flares up again, the cord, your wrists are torn, and you stagger backward, Grandma's not touching you now.

You manage to stay there, somehow you manage to stay there long enough to catch Grandma's smile. She doesn't say good-bye or see you later or Godspeed, there isn't the trace of a word. She gives you that smile because she has nothing more to give you and tonight there's not even a crumb of time left to you alone to be able to—

"Let's go," says the captain.

The hands obey at once, the hood covering you, closing your eyes in black, wrapping you one more time in the endless sticky suffocation of the cloth. Now you can't see your grandma, now you'll never see her again, not even once.

They push you and shove you and rough you up but you keep your feet, in the dark, there in front of the cell, facing what must still be your grandma's smile.

Under the smothering blindfold, praying for a little fresh air, you suddenly smell—oppressive, intense, an ocean penetrating, invading you—the other men who've been there, here. The other men. Hours and hours, weeks and months and years and hours of men, second by second, minutes, eyes, tongues, spit, sweat, hair, stains, salt, vomit, recriminations, betrayals, confusion, fear, that insufferable smell brewed by other men, supplications chewing this cloth before yours, eyes that tried to record a face like Grandma's or perhaps didn't even have that privilege, something, someone, anything, some last discernible light, some smile that won't be wiped out, they put it over every single one, one by one, minute by minute, one plus one plus one.

Then Alexis knew that Grandma was right. Even if she'd never said so, yes, she was right. He was going to survive.

You knew it like you knew that beyond the blindfold Grandma went on smiling in the darkness. You knew it better than if you were looking at her, better than if they'd taken that hood off, or if the captain had granted thousands of hours to talk before dawn.

Somebody shoves you brutally.

For a fraction of a fraction of a second, a second that delays and then melts away, you manage to hold yourself fast in front of the cell.

You move your head, already going, already on the way, lightly you nod, to say yes to Grandma or to say good-bye or for something else you don't know how to express any other way, and there's not even any light to see by, and you do it all the same because no one on earth will see you or be able to remember, going already, but it's good for you and you do it, that nod of the head in Grandma's direction. And then you set out walking down the corridor of your own free will.

It no longer mattered who said it, who whispered it way inside, so far inside, far off to the side.

He, Alexis, was going to survive.

I was going to the capital to find my father.

chapter eight

⸾ xii ⸾

A little before dawn, accompanied by his orderly, the captain arrived at the river.

"How are we doing, Lieutenant?" he asked, although by the flickering firelight he could already see him smiling. He'd never seen him grinning with such complacency.

"Fine, Captain, just fine. I was trained, I was born for this, not for talking all day long. And the kid?"

The captain started poking at the fire, stamping out a piece of wood that had managed to escape the flames. He noticed with fascination how the heat ate at his boot, the whistling and whipping of the fire blazing in the reflection of the boot's black leather as it stamped at the stubborn coal.

"Emmanuel," said the captain. "Tell the lieutenant."

"The prisoner has been dispatched. His grandmother didn't want to cooperate."

"That old woman mustn't have blood in her veins," the lieutenant remarked. "Cold as a snake."

"And stubborn as a mule. She saw the last man in her family being taken away and she didn't even say good-bye. I waited, to see what she'd do. But not a word. With people like that... Tell him, Emmanuel."

"There's not much more to tell, Captain."

The captain withdrew his boot from the fire when the heat became unbearable. The piece of wood hadn't moved. "With people like that..."

"I'm glad you see it that way, Captain."

"Everything in its time, Lieutenant. Now, even the priest will have to testify in our favor. We've done everything possible to save lives, explored every way out of this. Irreproachable conduct..." He noticed the lieutenant was aloof, unresponsive. He'd be thinking he always figured this was the only language these animals understood. A tough one, just like his father. To crack down halfway is worse than not at all. The only enemy that won't come back is the one we killed yesterday. Every little defenseless kid today will be a man tomorrow. He still remembered every sentence of the general in the military academy. The lieutenant's father will be happy now, when they inform him that finally, after so much negotiating, so many respectful attitudes and doves of peace and smiles for the defeated, that finally the only viable course had turned out to be the one he'd recommended, along with a group in the high command, since the beginning: force.

Suddenly the captain felt sick, with a weariness welling up from every fold in his body, merging with all the surrounding air, crushing in on him from the vague horizon of the hills. They all thought that: the general, the lieutenant, Gheorghakis, Kastoria, even the orderly, they all thought this effort had been pointless and, worse, doomed to fail. There were the bodies that someone was dumping with premeditated efficiency upriver, the bodies that would go on turning up later, perhaps by accident, in cesspools, ravines, crossroads, and they'd have to keep killing so that no one would ask where they came from, who'd put them there, why, how, how much longer. Deep down—and the captain wanted to obliterate the image, he wanted to wipe out the source of what was building inside him, the weariness that wasn't disgust, that would never be disgust, he wanted to negate what was deep down or the idea that a depth even existed—deep down, the only thing he really wanted was to go back home, open the door and find Nicola there and his three kids, to take off this skin that covered his body, turn himself inside out, trade these intestines for others, and have a nice Sunday with the family, for the family, and someday go back out to fight if necessary, but against armored divisions and airplanes and machine guns, a real war, without old ladies and little boys and half-grown girls. He looked at the lieutenant beside him, so satisfied, farther away than if he'd migrated to the other end of the universe, and he knew once more that he'd never be able to give him or so many others even the slightest hint of what had just happened to him and was now receding, squashed like a poisonous bug, fading away. He said, steadying his voice, "In any case, our instructions are the same. We resort to bullets only if we meet with violent resistance. Otherwise we proceed without fire. Those instructions come from higher up."

"Understood," said the lieutenant. "There's no point in wasting ammunition on these...women. Let's hope they don't start throwing rocks, eh?"

"Let's hope." The captain automatically pulled out his cigarette case. He was going to offer the lieutenant a cigarette, then remembered he didn't smoke. Same as his father. He stood looking at the cigarette case in his hand as if it were some strange and extravagant instrument whose exact use he couldn't be sure of. Why did he have it in his hand? Without opening it, he put it back in his pocket. "And them?" the captain asked.

The lieutenant pointed toward the thrashing but still invisible shore of the river. There they were, the same as yesterday and the day before, not moving, waiting...waiting for some miracle, some divine intervention, who knew what these crazy old women and their daughters were waiting for.

Over there, above the slow, gray dawn, a flock of birds crossed the sky, calling, formed in a graceful wedge against the high clouds, following their leader toward some destination beyond the mountains. The two officers and the orderly followed the flight of the birds, so radiant and soothing and clear, and the three of them felt strangely united in that moment. The captain thought that there overhead was something the women would also be watching, and maybe the boy on the truck headed for the capital and the rest of the soldiers, and he could understand why the lieutenant was waiting for the last bird to disappear, and the last echo in the pure air of the day that didn't want to begin but was on the verge of beginning anyway. The lieutenant waited till they were alone again in the silence, alone with the monotonous sound of the river, before calling out, "Form ranks, Sergeant." And then, more softly, "With your authorization, Captain."

The captain nodded. He saw how the soldiers lined up, creating a sort of human wall between him and the shore below. Beyond those backs he could just make out the group of women, in an opaque and foggy sort of way, some standing, others reclining or seated, next to the rocks. From that distance, and at that early hour, no shadow was individually distinguishable. Together they still formed a floating, savage mass, one huge spread-out female with fifteen or twenty heads. The captain noticed the absence of wind. Something told him that at a time like this there ought to be lots of wind, lots of air moving around and not settling.

"Atten*tion!*" the sergeant commanded.

The soldiers obeyed.

The sergeant signaled with his hand. "We're ready, Lieutenant."

"Perhaps, sir," suggested the lieutenant, "it would be advisable to give them one last warning."

The captain's voice didn't waver. "I don't see why, Lieutenant. They've had plenty of chances. They know what to expect."

"All right, Captain. If that's your opinion."

"As a matter of fact, Lieutenant, it is."

The soldiers began to move toward the beach.

Everything was hazy and barely clearing.

Suddenly the women came apart, split into two groups, the women opened up, and the captain could see the river, the beach, the rocks. A first ray of sunlight lit that spot, struck the air like a sword.

"Just a minute, Sergeant," said the captain.

The soldiers had stopped already.

There, among the women, was the body, the body of a third man the night and the river had deposited on that bank.